The Rose Engagement

Richard E. & Beverly A. Brown

Title:
The Rose Engagement

Authors:
Dr. Richard E. Brown and Beverly A. Brown

Kent Information Services, Inc.
155 N. Water St., Suite 205
Kent, OH 44240

http://www.kentis.com
email@kentis.com

+1 330.673.1300 voice
+1 330.673.6310 fax

In memory of Ken,
who gave us the idea
over 25 years ago.

This work is a novel, designed to show in an entertaining manner, the relevance and importance of accounting, especially governmental accounting, in the world about us. The accounting concepts, of course, are genuine. However, the story is fictional. While it was inspired by the events and places about us, no single person, place or event is the inspiration for the book, and no claim is made that the events described ever occurred, much less at the locations named.

Foreword

Shakespeare tells us that by any other name, a rose would smell as sweet. But he didn't read *The Rose Engagement*, a tale of felonious and treasonous intrigue in the White House that is by no means sweet. Fortunately for the country, Paul Sandler, a partner of an old-line Cleveland CPA firm, is the independent CPA with final responsibility for the audit of the White House staff operations, a CPA who soon finds himself enmeshed in some exciting nefarious doings.

Armed with his sense of ethics, command of auditing standards and knowledge of government accounting, blessed with a supportive and courageous spouse, aided by a senior partner with substantial wealth and unparalleled political contacts, Paul approaches the challenges of this unusual engagement with the dogged persistence and professional skepticism of a competent auditor.

Thus, it is no surprise that murder and mayhem do not deter him from the completion of his audit, to the everlasting gratitude of his fellow citizens. At last, a CPA who is a hero!

The Rose Engagement illustrates how important it is for ordinary people involved in the accounting function of a government unit, or any entity, to perform their work carefully—not doing so, as the reader will see, can lead to some very unpleasant consequences. And it illustrates how everyone, no matter what they do, should be alert to the possibility that their employer or their colleagues might be involved in a situation involving fraud, illegal acts, or worse. Finally, it illustrates how good old generally accepted auditing standards are still relevant as a framework for applying the more specialized knowledge an auditor must have to perform a government audit engagement effectively and efficiently—and in compliance with GAO standards.

Every novel, it is said, must have some sex, but this one does not because Paul, recognizing his obligations as an auditor (and, one would hope, his duty to his spouse), avoids a situation with a *femme fatale* that might impair the appearance of his independence. Readers today might wish that everyone involved in government possessed the same moral rectitude.

Although the very name of the book might cause some to think it is based on current developments, it is not. The plot draws on a wide range of fictional circumstances. Some made me think of the White House of

Woodrow Wilson, for example, so there is little danger that this book will be seen as another *Primary Colors*.

In my opinion, people interested in accounting and auditing will find the book worthwhile. I found it an easy read and one that was enjoyable and educational as well. Of course, I was involved in setting standards for CPAs for many years and now act as a consultant and expert witness on those standards—others may need more excitement to really turn them on. But try it anyway. I think you'll like it.

Thomas P. Kelley, CPA
New York
76711.1551@compuserve.com

Preface

Government accounting and auditing are exciting and challenging. Unfortunately, current literature does not always convey this excitement. As a result, the public and even those considering careers in government auditing and accounting often do not appreciate either (1) the dynamic world of government accountants and auditors or (2) the important contribution that government accountants and auditors make to the process of democratic government. We have written ***The Rose Engagement*** to help bridge this gap between public perception and the lively realm in which government accountants and auditors actually operate.

A number of highly regarded individuals with extensive teaching and practical experience were kind enough to review this novel. We wish to thank Michael Pearson, an outstanding professor of auditing at Kent State

University, and Jack Tucker, a retired KPMG Peat Marwick partner and visiting professor at Kent State University. We also received helpful critiques from several practitioners, including Mark Funkhauser, City Auditor of Kansas City, Missouri; William Thomson in the Arizona Office of the Auditor General; and Ronald Points in Price Waterhouse's Office of Government Services in Washington, D.C. Our three grown children, Kelly, Christopher, and Kirsten, an attorney, a physician, and a college student, respectively, also provided invaluable insights. The personnel at Kent Information Services, Inc., including John and Penny Graves, Christine McGill, and Jacqueline Justice, provided extensive, substantive editorial review. We sincerely thank all these individuals.

Richard E. Brown
Beverly A. Brown

The Rose Engagement

1

Jim Foley had been working as an accountant on the White House staff for only a few days. He looked up from his desk, smiling as he scanned the busy office. The thrill of working for the White House was still sharp for Jim. Apparently, his predecessor had not shared that enthusiasm; he had left abruptly, giving Jim minimal training or guidance, and a lot of work to do.

Jim forced himself to focus on his work. He was processing payments for a number of vouchers that had come to the office. Some items were to be paid from "private," "outside," or "donated" funds, accounted for in various trust funds. Others would be passed on to Treasury, with appropriate documentation, for payment from the General Fund. Unfortunately, Jim did not know which vouchers were to be paid from which funds. He may have received instructions on this important matter, but in the rush to fill the position, his training on these details had been incomplete. In any event, he was unsure how to proceed and did not know who would be able to help him.

Jim looked around the office again, and walked to a neighboring desk. “Mary, have you ever processed the paperwork for paying bills that come to the office?”

“No way,” Mary responded quickly without even looking up from her work. “Catherine’s the only one who ever did that, and she’s long gone on vacation.”

A young man, sitting at another desk nearby, had been listening and suggested, “Do the best you can, Jim. There are only a few bills Catherine would have paid from trust funds. Once you learn the ropes you can always make it right later by running through a correction and, say, repay the general fund with trust fund dollars.”

Jim returned to his desk and looked again at the pile of paperwork before him. He sighed as he glanced around the office bustling with people who seemed so efficient and so sure of their jobs. He knew that he could wait—there was so much work to do that he could certainly fill his time until Catherine returned to give him the necessary training. But Jim did not want to wait. He wanted to be efficient, to take advantage of discounts available from vendors. He wanted to prove that he could take initiative, prove that he belonged on the White House accounting staff.

Jim turned his attention back to the paperwork before him. From the top of the pile of vouchers he picked up some bills from a florist in Phoenix, Arizona, unusual expenditures for the White House. Jim glanced at the vouchers and then sent them on to the Department of the Treasury for payment from regular government funds. After all, he could correct any errors later, and there was so much work to do. And it was only a small bill for a few roses.

2

When Dodney, Harrison and Co-partners, Certified Public Accountants, had told Stephanie Hamilton she was to be the lead field person on the firm's audit of the White House staff operations—yes, the White House—naturally, she was thrilled. This was just the kind of assignment which could propel a senior or "heavy" manager into firm partnership, and at the early age of twenty-nine at that. While not exactly one of the "Big 6" of the public accounting profession, Dodney, Harrison was still one of Cleveland's oldest, largest and most prestigious firms. Besides, the pay was great, especially for partners. And the firm was keeping a sharp eye out for prospective female partners.

As she waited for the staff meeting about the Washington engagement to begin, Stephanie Hamilton reflected upon why she had decided upon a career in public accounting. She had been a good, solid B plus student at Kent State University. Her enthusiasm and involvement in professional activities, including Beta Alpha Psi and the Accounting Association, had made her an attractive, prospective employee. She had "cast her net" fairly wide, looking at many diverse career opportunities, including internal auditing, commercial/industrial accounting, the U.S. General Accounting Office and State Auditor's Office, a large area hospital, consulting and public accounting.

After choosing to try public accounting for a few years, she had decided she was better suited for a regional CPA firm. Stefie knew she might not like the demands associated with an international firm—travel and probable relocations. ("Stefie" was the name she preferred to go by. Her nickname annoyed her parents. "If we wanted a daughter named 'Stefie,'" her father would say, "you'd see it on your birth certificate!", but it suited her—simple and friendly.) Her friends, parents and fiancé lived in Ohio, and she wanted to stay close. It was beginning to appear she had made a good decision. She had taken and passed the CPA exam, and with this hurdle behind her, her future at Dodney, Harrison and Co-partners seemed bright.

As the staff members gathered, Stefie reviewed her notes. The engagement was an important one to her firm, and she meant to complete the assignment competently. The current administrators in the White House were anxious to demonstrate that they could keep their own house in order, and so had sought an outside audit of their finances and operations. This move seemed politically astute since there was currently considerable pressure from the business community and public at large to improve the Federal government's financial practices. After some hurried and informal talks with contacts in the GAO, White House staff people had recommended that they go for the "whole thing": a comprehensive audit that would include a financial statement audit and a performance audit. However, under the contract and engagement letter they were to be performed sequentially, and the performance phase would be dependent upon successful completion of the financial audit on a timely basis and within the agreed upon budget for fees and expenses. The audit package had been competitively bid, but in this case the White House chose not to select the lowest bidder. Instead, as the engagement proposal allowed, they had selected the second lowest bidder—Dodney, Harrison—based on the firm's extensive experience in governmental and performance work. The administration, in addition to being anxious to involve private firms in governmental affairs, also wanted to involve medium-sized and smaller firms. Dodney, Harrison was one of the beneficiaries of these policies. Of course, the fact that old Sidney Harrison, as in Dodney, Harrison, was a buddy of several administration officials, hadn't hurt either.

As the meeting started, Stefie rose and said in a clear, unwavering voice, "I want you to know how much I appreciate this assignment. I will do my best for the firm. You can rest assured of that. Whatever it takes."

"Yes, yes," said John Ryan, one of the sterner of the several partners in attendance. "If we didn't believe that, you wouldn't be here today. But you must understand the political dimensions of this engagement. It could help the firm, and you, a great deal. We certainly didn't go after this one for the fee."

"We'll be lucky to cover travel, living, and other engagement expenses, let alone salaries," muttered another partner.

"I don't know much about these governmental audits, but I know they can consume staff hours like 'The Blob,'" continued Ryan. "I also know they can be controversial. In the late 1980s we landed what we thought was a dynamite opportunity in Pennsylvania, a special review of that state's Medicaid program. Seems they had gotten into a tremendous squabble with their fiscal agent, the company that administers the program and processes all claims. As I recall it, we were looking at about $300,000 in fees and $100,000 in expenses to figure out what went wrong. We thought a quick review of the contract and a brief report ought to do it, but as the rest of the people in this room will remember, many months later we were sandwiched in between lawsuits by the state against the fiscal agent, the agent against the state, and some thoughts on both sides about suing us!"

Paul Sandler, another partner and the partner-in-charge of this new Washington engagement spoke up at this point, "John, as you well know, I directed that engagement at the time and, like Stefie, was a 'heavy manager.' Every time you tell that story you neglect to add that we did not get sued by anyone, brought the engagement in within the budgeted hours and costs, and wrote a very special add-on contract for litigation support work. Having said all that, I acknowledge how difficult such audits can be."

"Let's get to the point," interjected still another partner with his own ideas about the job. "We want you to get in and get out, Stefie. Stay within the project budget, a loser at best. We want the experience, the presence for our firm. Paul has helped us build up a fine governmental practice, and this engagement will continue that growth in a very positive way."

As the partners left the meeting Stefie waited outside for Paul. She wanted to talk over the engagement one more time. Paul, the firm's authority on these kinds of government audits, had always been willing to help Stefie, and she was counting on his support and advice now.

Paul smiled at Stefie and nodded in the direction of his office. As they walked together down the hall, Stefie said, "No one has shared the engagement contract with me yet, Paul, so I'm not entirely clear as to the scope of this assignment. You know that most of my experience is in the banking area and this will be the largest government audit that I have managed."

"Sorry, I'll ask Ann to leave it on your desk. Don't worry, Stefie, you are ready for this engagement. You are our best manager. Our engagement contract calls for us to follow generally accepted government auditing standards as contained in the *Government Auditing Standards*, the *Yellow Book* and issued by the Comptroller General of the U.S., who, of course, heads the GAO. Nothing out of the ordinary. The relevant auditing standards of the American Institute of Certified Public Accountants have been incorporated into the *Yellow Book*, but the *Yellow Book* adds additional standards in such areas as compliance with laws and regulations, illegal acts, materiality, and internal controls."

Stefie nodded as Paul continued, "Our engagement calls for us to perform a financial statement audit as delineated in the *Yellow Book*. Therefore, under this first portion of the engagement you must determine whether the financial statements of the entity present fairly the financial position, results of operations, and cash flows in accordance with generally accepted accounting principles, or GAAP."

"But who is the entity in this case, Paul? The President? The government?" asked Stefie.

"It's much simpler than that, Stefie. In this case, the entity is defined in the contract as the immediate White House office and staff. The toughest part of this audit will be the compliance portion. We must determine whether the office has complied with relevant laws and regulations. This compliance element is a very important aspect of audit because if it isn't done just right, it can consume lots of time and create other problems. We must carefully review the entity's control structure. And, finally, we must report on each of these areas. There are also other reporting requirements unique to governmental audits."

"OK," agreed Stefie. "Assuming the first part of the engagement goes as planned, what happens next?"

Paul continued, "Our contract then calls for us to continue with a performance audit of White House operations, including travel, procurement, printing, payroll, work flow, use of space, and the like. The White House Office employs about 400 full-time equivalent workers and has an annual budget of about $42 million annually. While not large by Federal government standards, the strategic placement of the organization makes the audit very important. Again, the *Yellow Book* pretty clearly spells out our charge here. We are to look at economy and efficiency, including use of resources, causes of any inefficient practices and, again, we must check for compliance with the laws and regulations in this area, such as following proper practices like using the competitive bidding process where needed, obtaining reasonable charges for travel, and so on. Lastly, the contract also requires us to consider program results or benefits of activities and, again, legal compliance is an important consideration."

"So," replied Stefie, "in the context of what is basically an office staff operation, I suppose I would consider, for example, whether the travel office gets people where they need to be on time and at a reasonable cost, and whether printing is completed on a timely basis and at a reasonable cost. If not, I would need to ask why not, and perhaps suggest options such as contracting out the function to a private company or to other parts of the government."

Paul nodded as Stefie spoke, "You've got it. It's an exciting and challenging engagement, Stefie. A chance to really make a contribution, make some money, build the firm's reputation. And it won't hurt your career any either."

Smiling, Stefie responded, "Thanks Paul. I'll do my best. See you when I get back from Washington."

3

Stefie meant what she had said. She would do her best. But now three weeks later, sitting in her office in the White House, she was concerned. What had started as a career-building assignment had quickly turned into an unmitigated pain in the neck. Stefie Hamilton had badly underestimated the amount of time she would personally need to spend on the job in Washington. She had mistakenly assumed that she would play a key role in planning the engagement and exercise general supervision, and that a cadre of younger, less experienced members of the audit staff would do most of the actual on-site work, including the interviewing, and the testing and checking of White House and other records. Unfortunately for Stefie, the partners of Dodney, Harrison believed this audit might lead to other important engagements, and so they wanted Stefie to remain on-site most of the time. The sensitivity of the engagement had dictated that other, experienced personnel were being used too, but she was completing much of the on-site work herself.

As the engagement progressed, Stefie had started to realize that she had not asked enough good, tough questions about the engagement, and about the special application of the auditing standards to government situations. The issue of who her client was, continued to trouble her. Who was the entity whose control structure should be examined? While it could be argued that the President was the client, his special assistant had signed the contract for the White House, and Stefie had yet to meet him.

Even the details of personal interaction in this Washington engagement were problematic. She and other staff members had been given obviously inferior White House office space and no clerical support. It was bad enough she had to be on-site so much, doing much of the audit work herself; but now she was having trouble finding places for her staff members to sit, work, and make phone calls. The President's staff people had not been very helpful. While Stefie Hamilton was not altogether certain who she was dealing with, she had a pretty good idea her contacts were far removed from the President. Although the White House staff tried to imply quite the opposite, Stefie had concluded, "They probably wouldn't know the President if they bumped into him."

This morning, Stefie had run a sample of payments with a cut-off of $5,000. The sample included a couple of unusual entries, including a payment of several thousand dollars to a Phoenix florist for roses. Under normal circumstances, she would pay no attention to such small items. But since they had popped up in her sample of general fund expenditures, Stefie was obligated to audit the supporting documentation. Besides, it was strange, not at all the kind of thing for which governmental funds would normally be used. So far, she had been unable to find supporting documentation for the transactions, and the White House staff had been uncooperative. Stefie was considering calling in her colleagues from the Cleveland office to ask for their intervention. She knew, however, that she must take such an action only as a last recourse, since it could reflect poorly on her as partnership material.

Only Rob Fenna, one of the assistants to the Special Assistant to the President, took any interest at all, and his was a very negative one. After grudgingly allowing her into his office, he listened impatiently as Stefie asked about the transaction.

"Look," Fenna barked, "we didn't hire Dodney, Harrison to chase down the purchase of a bunch of daisies in the desert country. I'm not about to go to my boss, a Special Assistant to the President of the United States, and question him about a bunch of flowers someone bought many months ago. He'd have me locked up, but only after he canned me."

Much of Rob Fenna's reaction was pure overkill, his typical knee-jerk response when uncomfortably cornered. Fenna worried about Stephanie's questions after she had left his office; as he matched Stephanie's rather simple questions with other information he had recently and accidentally seen, he became more and more troubled. He made two phone calls. The first was to his boss, the Special Assistant to the President. Then, possibly to protect himself, he called a newspaper contact.

That same day, Frank Norman, the Special Assistant to the President, called Stefie to his office to talk over the progress of the audit. During the first few weeks of the audit, he had been unavailable to Stefie. But now, Norman seemed to show an inordinate interest in the technical and ethical aspects of an audit. Stefie, on the defensive after her meeting with Rob Fenna, handled each question with the kind of response which had gotten her through the CPA exam.

"Why horse around with such a petty amount of money, Ms. Hamilton? We must spend millions daily just in our little part of the Federal government."

"Yes, that's so; but auditing standards dictate that I must verify each item kicked out by my procedures. That's even more true when the transactions are out of the ordinary. In retrospect, perhaps my $5,000 threshold was a bit low, but I used my professional judgment and made that decision. I can't simply change my mind now without undermining the integrity of the audit."

Norman pressed on, becoming more testy, "What, specifically, do you want, Ms. Hamilton? Exactly what kind of money are we talking about here?"

"I'm trying to find the original invoice or invoices, or some other documentation, for the purchase of a little over $5,000 of roses during the past fiscal year," responded Stefie. "There may be more money involved. I'm not sure just yet, and I may need to expand my test work to find out. There is more than just the issue of the total amount of the payments; roses are unusual items to be paid from the general fund, using public monies."

"For God's sake," Frank Norman protested, "the Federal government now has a budget of about a trillion-and-a-half dollars, and we've got to come up with the original purchase orders for $5,000 worth of flowers! I've served the President for many years. Long before he was President, when he was Attorney General and then Vice President. Even before that. I've been around this city a long time, and I've never heard anything like this."

Unaccustomed to such a blatant show of authority, and seeing her partnership hopes waning, Stefie worked hard to stay cool. "I'm afraid that's what you paid us for. That's what our profession requires. First of all, we're not auditing the U.S. Government on this engagement, and so the size of the budget is impressive but irrelevant, Mr. Norman. We were hired to conduct an audit of a very small part of the government, the White House Office. Our contract is clear on that."

Stefie continued, "I don't mean to give you a lecture on auditing, Mr. Norman, but this kind of situation is covered pretty well by the very auditing standards you wrote into our agreement. First of all, the General Standards discuss something called due professional care, calling for the use of sound judgment—and I emphasize judgment—in establishing audit scope, selecting methodology, and choosing tests and procedures. Yes, it's true that the auditor must consider materiality and significance, that is, the potential impact of the item or items on the financial statements in designing the testwork, but..."

"See," Norman interrupted, "that's precisely my point. $5,000 worth of daisies doesn't amount to much in a budget this size!"

"But," continued Stefie, "in determining materiality the auditor must look beyond the monetary value of the item alone. Again, professional judgment must be exercised, and qualitative factors must be weighed. Such qualitative factors might include the cumulative impact of immaterial items. And there's more. Management's compliance with applicable laws and regulations also enters in. And, finally, it is recognized that materiality levels may be set lower in the case of governmental audits."

Norman was silent for a moment. He then used a ploy all too familiar to the auditor — the delaying tactic. "I'll do what I can to figure this out," he promised, "but don't hold your breath. It will take some time."

"I understand that, Mr. Norman. However, you need to understand that I can't wind up my work until this matter is resolved. As I understand our engagement contract, our firm will first construct and then offer an opinion on your immediate office's financial statements, and only those of your immediate office. Assuming all goes well, we may then continue work. Stage two of the engagement will be a performance audit, a review of certain efficiency and effectiveness elements of your operations. My firm must, therefore, render an opinion on your financial statements, which you wish to use as something of an example to other parts of the government. It is clear I must resolve all open items, including this one. If that means a trip to Phoenix, it will have to be done. Also, unless I can rather quickly obtain an explanation about this problem, I may, under the standards, need to expand my field work. I could be exposing myself and my firm (*and my partnership,* Stefie thought) to considerable risk if I do a half-baked job on this audit. Moreover, you would doubt our ability to conduct the following stages of the audit."

The Special Assistant to the President claimed to understand what Stephanie was talking about. As a lawyer, he said, he knew how "tied in you could get, chasing down the smallest detail simply because some obscure book said you should." He congratulated Stephanie on her hard work and the progress she had made, shaking her hand firmly as she left the office. While flattered, Stefie was smart enough and skeptical enough (after all, she was a good auditor) to feel uneasy.

Why, she pondered, *all the sudden attention to a lowly accountant who couldn't get adequate office space a few hours earlier? This rose purchase is starting to look more like an irregularity than just an error.*

Stephanie Hamilton worked late that night, as she had most nights during this Washington engagement. The long hours away from home, her fiancé, and her family had quickly dimmed the thrill of being in the nation's capital. Accounting records were the same, after all, whether on a Cleveland bank audit or an audit of the White House. She now wanted to simply complete the job as rapidly as possible and return to Cleveland. "But," she added aloud, "complete it successfully, which means getting phase one done right and not losing the second part of the engagement."

As she was completing her day's work, Mike Antonio stuck his head through her doorway. Mike was one of the several firm members assigned to the engagement. A senior auditor, he had a pretty solid track record in government and nonprofit work. He also had an eye for Stefie, and Stefie knew it.

"Hey, Stefie, we're all going to get some dinner. How about joining us?"

"Thanks, Mike, but I have some things I need to finish up. You all go ahead."

"Well, then, why don't I drop by your place later on so we can kick around the audit?"

Smiling, Stefie responded, "Give it up, Mike, you know I'm engaged. And close the door on your way out."

Before quitting for the evening, Stefie wanted to document her day's activities and concerns. Indeed, the field work standards for financial audits, under evidence, make it clear that a record of the auditor's work must be retained in the form of working papers, including sufficient information to enable another experienced auditor, having no previous connection with the audit, to follow the evidence supporting the conclusions and judgments. So Stefie wrote down, in summary form, her meetings, conversations, and concerns. Then she faxed these most recent pages of notes to the secretary at the Cleveland office she shared with Paul Sandler. She also made a decision to discuss all this with Paul as soon as possible.

The other staff members had left a little after six p.m. It was dark and after nine o'clock when Stefie finished for the day. She was still thinking over the day's events as she walked along 16th Street, not far from the White House, en route to the small apartment she had taken nearby. As she walked, she tried to clear her thoughts of the day's concerns. A bubble bath and a phone call to her fiancé were all she had on her mind now.

She didn't even notice the van when it turned the corner. Traveling at an incredible speed, the van actually came onto the sidewalk to run her down. For fear that the young accountant might survive this first crushing blow, the wild driver actually slammed on his brakes, put the car in reverse and backed over Stefie again at high speed. The van then sped off and disappeared into the night.

The people who did see the accident saw few, if any, helpful details. It was an old, dark van. The rear license plate, should anyone have thought to note it, was in darkness with the plate light out.

4

Peter Wilson had just finished supper when the phone rang. He tensed when he heard the apologetic tone in his managing editor's voice, "Pete, got one for you that doesn't seem like much and may turn out to be nothing. But then again, you've been around enough to know you never know."

Peter Wilson was really ticked off. He knew he wasn't the world's greatest journalist, but he was with *The Washington Globe* and had been doing a pretty good job for several years now. He deserved better treatment than this, he thought. "Cut the stuff, John, and tell me the bad news. If it were a good assignment, you'd be delivering the news face-to-face. Now just where am I going this time?"

For the typical *Globe* staffer, leaving Washington

(except, maybe, for a New York assignment) was tantamount to being banished. After all, for a political writer the action was in the District. Even Peter Wilson's years of experience did not make him more willing to spend several days in the desert.

"Pete," Barlow had said, "I want you to go to Phoenix."

"The one in Arizona?"

"Yes, the one in Arizona! We got a tip yesterday from a White House staffer. Claims he has seen strange payments for transactions in Phoenix for all kinds of weird things. Staff salaries, lease payments, medical bills, medicines, and so on. They seem centered around a new resort on the outskirts of town. It is probably nothing, but I'm not about to ignore a White House tip. At the very least, I've got to tell my contact we checked it out, if we want him to continue to help. Also, I want a good and experienced reporter to look into it."

Wilson thanked the managing editor in the style to which his friend—yes, really his friend—had grown accustomed, including all of the usual colorful expletives. Then, knowing full well that Barlow was right, he gathered up the little available information passed on by the White House contact, made his plane and hotel reservations, and left the next morning from Washington National Airport for "the desert."

Peter Wilson really wasn't much of an investigative

reporter. He could cover and write up a political event with the best of them, but he hadn't spent much time as a snoop—studying complex and detailed files, locating and interviewing reluctant, even hostile witnesses, etc. Frankly, he was uncomfortable with such a role and wasn't altogether sure that it was a legitimate activity for a reporter.

Well, Wilson thought, *if it could make Woodward and Bernstein rich and famous, who am I to get uppity? And besides, I've never been to Arizona.*

Wilson's initial contacts in Phoenix had not gone well at all. He visited a Dr. Alfred Holstein, whose name appeared on a couple of the documents copied and passed on to *The Globe* by the White House staffer. The physician, while obviously impressed by such a visit, was nonetheless reticent.

"Yes," Holstein had stated in PR fashion, "I visit several elderly patients who live in a retirement and resort community called The Peake, and who cannot come to see me. That's the kind of practice I wish to have. I go back many years with some of these patients. My financial position is such that money is not an issue."

Wilson interrupted the speech, "I think that's great. God knows, I wish my own doctor would follow your lead. But I am primarily interested in one patient. A Mr. Harold T. Johnson. I've come across documents which show that you have been visiting him quite a lot over the past few months, and you've received one or two payments from regular government funds. Could... "

The physician's professional code shot to the fore, "Mr. Wilson, I care for many patients, some elderly, some at The Peake, with payments coming from many different sources. I worked in Washington many years ago and that could account for..." Dr. Holstein changed directions. "We must assume those payments are legitimate. I understand you are trying to do your job—though I don't fully understand it—but I can not divulge to you any details of my care for a specific patient."

Wilson continued, "You worked in Washington? May I ask in what capacity?"

"Mr. Wilson, I think I've told you everything I know pertinent to this matter. I wish you well. Good day."

As Peter Wilson left Dr. Holstein's office, he wondered about the physician's Washington connections and sensed that Dr. Holstein would tell someone about this conversation the minute he left. As he started his car, Wilson laughed at his own paranoia, muttering, "Too many James Bond movies," as he turned on the radio and drove away.

As the reporter made his way around the city, his attention turned to the desert heat, "This is one hot city. I'll kill Barlow when I see him. Or at least I'll beat his tail at poker next week and love every minute of it."

The Phoenix temperature was hitting 107, and Peter Wilson wasn't buying the local PR about the low humidity and the resulting not-so-bad "comfort factor." He had been all over town in this heat, and he was miserable and no closer to finding the answers to his questions.

To trace the prescriptions on the copied documents his editor had given him, Wilson visited drugstores that were all over the Phoenix metropolitan area. The pharmacist who seemed to have the biggest and most active business was confused, having difficulty understanding why *The Washington Globe* cared about Mr. Harold Johnson's drug bills.

"We're impeaching a Governor and putting him on trial and you Eastern papers hardly cover it. Who's Harold Johnson?"

Wilson tried to ingratiate himself a bit to the man, agreeing, "You're right there, we should do better on covering such stories. And frankly, I don't know who Harold Johnson is. Do you? What does he buy, and how often?"

"I've never seen the man. Let me check my records," commented the pharmacist as he scrolled through his computer records. "No big deal here. A few prescriptions filled each month. No unusual drugs or doses. Yeah, the checks seem to have recently started to come from a different government account, but they are regular. There are so many of those government bodies now you don't notice unless the checks bounce. At least they pay. I believe a number of different people pick up the prescriptions. I can't remember anyone in particular."

The visit to the state government offices was a joke, *a hot one*, Wilson thought to himself. He studied the bureaucrat who stood to shake his hand, *This guy looks like a bureaucrat! What's worse, he acts like one!*

Wilson swallowed his irritation, wiped the sweat from his forehead and smiled, "How do you do, sir. I've been referred to your office. I'm from *The Washington Globe...*"

"Washington State?" asked the bureaucrat.

"No, DC—and I'm trying to find out about some Federal government checks sent to pay the medical bills of a Mr. Harold Johnson who resides at The Peake."

"I'll bet the State Controller's Office sent you," suggested the bureaucrat suspiciously.

"No, they didn't," Wilson assured the man.

"Well, then who did send you? The State Auditor General's Office? The Attorney General's Office?"

"No."

"I know, another one of those legislative committees?"

"No," Wilson stated firmly. "Does it matter who sent me? All I want is a little information."

"Look, pal,..." sensing there was no political clout

behind the visitor, the bureaucrat actually seemed to grow in stature and his voice became more sure, "Let's start over. Who are you and what do you want?"

Wilson repeated his tale.

The bureaucrat relaxed and smiled. He was riding high now, invincible. No investigation. No legislative inquiry. Simply a chance to dazzle a reporter with the department's computer wizardry. In a flash, several dozen Harold T. Johnsons were on his screen. Within a few minutes, the list was narrowed to one at The Peake. One lone entry, in which the Arizona state government, for some inexplicable reason, had kicked in through its version of the Medicaid program to help pay for a series of tests for Mr. Johnson.

"No, I can't say what kind of tests we helped pay for. But Johnson—assuming it is your Mr. Johnson—lives at 701 Wagon Wheel at The Peake. Odd that the State would help someone living at that pricey address, but hey, I just work here."

"What a price to pay for an address," muttered Wilson as he left the bureaucrat behind. "I swear I'll bring in card sharks to make sure Barlow never wins a hand of cards again."

Peter Wilson checked his documents. Only one more stop to make—May's Flowers.

The flower shop was a long way from downtown Phoenix where he had his discussion with the unnamed bureaucrat. But at least the visit to the florist was one that seemed to pay off—or so it seemed to a non-investigative, investigative reporter.

"Hi, I'm Peter Wilson, and I'm trying to settle the final affairs of a Mr. Harold Johnson. He lives at 701 Wagon Wheel at The Peake. He's been buying a lot of flowers from you lately, and I want to be sure all those bills have been paid. Will you help me?"

Peter Wilson was learning. Not much to this investigative reporting stuff after all.

"Sure, I'll help," responded a young woman who was obviously a part-time employee. This seemed more interesting to her than arranging and selling flowers. "Let me check our records. Wow! That guy must like flowers. Looks like he had a single rose delivered every day for a long, long time. Several years. But they're all paid for. No problem, except that we received a note telling us to stop delivery just several days ago."

"Do your records show who actually paid for the flowers?"

"I'm not sure," replied the young woman. "There are a few notes here on the account card. Seems some unusual checks came in recently from the Federal government to pay the bill. Before that the checks came from a different government source, and some years earlier from some group called the Evergreen Society, located in Washington, DC. That's the group that recently sent the final note and a check to pay the balance. Doesn't say anything more."

Wilson's investigatory skills were sharpening. "Are you sure it doesn't say anything more about that private Society?"

"No, it doesn't."

"Could I speak to the individual who actually delivered all those roses?"

The florist-in-training responded by shouting to a man (who Peter assumed was the owner, manager or both) in an adjacent room, "Bill, a gentleman here wants to talk to Bob Mileson. He around?"

"Where you been?" came the response, presumably from Bill. "He quit a week ago. Seems he came into some money and left town. Who wants to know about him?"

With hurried and flimsy excuses, Wilson beat a hasty retreat. He needed time to think. This was an important find, and he'd need to follow up in the right way, at the right time. He went back to his hotel, had a cup of coffee, and considered his next step. He pulled out a map and decided to head up to The Peake.

Wilson learned that finding one's way around Phoenix was easy to plan, but difficult to execute. The streets are laid out in a nice checkerboard fashion, so finding The Peake was not a serious problem. Actually getting there, however, was another matter, since Phoenix expressways were clogged with construction projects. The result was that the trip to The Peake, only twenty miles south of Phoenix, took a long time.

By the time Peter Wilson arrived at The Peake it was after dark and he was hungry. He pulled into a small restaurant to have supper and to figure out how much more time he would have to spend in Phoenix. While he was eating, he decided to try to finish up his business as soon as possible and return home. Maybe he could catch an early morning flight. Unfortunately, it would be too late once he completed his work tonight to get on a "red-eye" and be in Washington tomorrow at a decent hour.

The Peake was isolated mostly by virtue of being located on a mountain side. As near as he could tell in the darkness, 701 Wagon Wheel was one of those beautiful western-type, large, modern homes, located close to the center of the resort. Wilson had thought long and hard about checking with the phone company and phoning first, but had finally decided a surprise visit might be more fruitful. He parked along the street a few doors from the house he wanted. Although there was little traffic, he did not notice the car with its headlights off that quietly pulled in forty or fifty yards behind him.

By now the reporter's instincts and imagination, or some strange blend of the two, were in high gear. Why would the U.S. government, and at one time, a private foundation, pay for medical bills, flowers, and who knows what else for a Harold T. Johnson? A foreign dictator on the lam? Some key witness who will testify against the underworld? There were many possibilities and all were intriguing. And a bit scary. Wilson reminded himself to phone Washington to bring Barlow up to date after this last meeting. "If I die of dehydration from this desert weather, all my work will have been wasted," he muttered to himself as he left his car and approached the house.

Instead of going straight to the front door and ringing the bell, he began to quietly circle the house, peeking in windows. As he peered through a rear window, moving his face close to the glass, he heard a movement behind him. Before he could turn, a muscular arm closed over him. He could not move. Peter Wilson struggled to free himself from the arms of his attacker. He couldn't see his attacker's face, but Wilson did notice a ring set with a large turquoise stone on his attacker's hand, before he blacked out.

A short distance away from this residential area is the real resort area of The Peake—apartments, restaurants, tennis courts and swimming pools. A well-known feature of The Peake's main swimming pool is its swim-up bar, for those who cannot decide whether they want to drink or swim. This bar separates the regular bar and the actual swimming pool.

The next morning a few early partying swimmers found themselves sharing the swim-up bar with Peter Wilson's submerged dead body. James Thompson from Ottawa saw him first and nearly drowned gulping his

Bloody Mary. An autopsy showed that Peter Wilson had drowned, and there was no evidence of alcohol, other than some wine at dinner time. Death by water in the desert country—an ironic end. And that's the way *The Washington Globe* concluded its story on Peter Wilson's death.

5

But that is not what John Barlow, editor of *The Washington Globe*, concluded. Barlow had been assured by the Phoenix police that no evidence existed to indicate that Peter Wilson's death was anything but an accident. But Barlow couldn't believe that his friend and skilled reporter could just slip and drown accidentally while on assignment. Barlow needed more solid information about what happened to Peter, but he was getting nothing from the Phoenix police. Barlow thought, *Peter must have accidentally uncovered something big enough for someone to want to keep him permanently quiet. But what?* Barlow kept staring at a faxed copy of the thin police report—*it just couldn't have been an accident. Could it?*

The phone rang. It was one of John's newest reporters. "Mr. Barlow, I've got something I thought you should know right away."

"Go ahead," replied John.

"Last night, I was at the scene of a hit and run accident—thought it might prove interesting since it was less than a half mile from the White House."

"Go on," sighed Barlow impatiently.

"Well, the accident was common enough, except that the victim was Stephanie Hamilton. Ring any bells, Mr. Barlow?"

"Not at the moment, Saul. Please continue."

"Well, this morning I remembered how Peter complained to me about the assignment you gave him before he left. Said that you were sending him on a wild goose chase—had to investigate some tips given to you by a White House staffer. He also mentioned that some of the information he got from you was dredged up by an ongoing audit of the White House office. Peter said it was real petty stuff. But, anyway, the woman who was run down was the CPA in charge of that very same audit."

Barlow bit his lower lip and said in a very controlled voice, "Get whatever information you can gather about the accident—I mean everything, and then give your report directly to me. You are not to answer any questions about this investigation to anyone. Got it?"

"Sure, Mr. Barlow, whatever you want."

"Saul?"

"Yes, Mr. Barlow."

"Good work, son."

"Thank you, Mr Barlow."

John hung up the phone and secretly prayed that this rookie reporter would do exactly as he asked. He could send a more experienced person to the scene, but he didn't want to give too much attention to this accident. Sending his best people to investigate a simple hit-and-run could tip someone off that he suspected that it was more than a simple accident. If no one suspected that he was investigating Peter Wilson's death, he could buy the time he desperately needed to go over all that had occurred in the last 24 hours.

Barlow shook his head in bewilderment, and thought, *two people dead on the same night researching the same thing in two different parts of the country. What in the world is going on?* Now John Barlow had no doubt that Peter Wilson was murdered.

6

Paul Sandler was in the middle of teaching a continuing professional education session for about a dozen Dodney, Harrison staff members when Tom Spivey, the firm's partner-in-charge of audit services, came quietly into the training room and stood silently. He had just received the news about Stefie Hamilton and wanted to tell Paul immediately. However, he knew how much Paul enjoyed these training sessions—talking about his favorite topics, governmental and nonprofit accounting and auditing. Realizing Paul was in the middle of a session, he decided to wait until he had finished. And so he left the room as quietly as he entered, determined to return at the session's close.

Paul always made certain he reminded his classes of the continuing education requirements in the *Yellow Book*. Auditors involved in government audits had to complete at least 80 hours of training every two years. At least 20 hours had to be completed in any one year, and 24 of the 80 hours were to be in subjects directly related to the government environment and auditing. Dodney, Harrison tried to ensure that this requirement was met by providing some in-house training sessions for most staff members. More senior members of the firm received at least a part of their required hours by attending seminars and conferences around the state and even out-of-state. Paul often shared some of the sessions on governmental accounting and auditing with one or two professors from neighboring colleges and universities, but today's session was one he normally taught alone.

"Remember," he was telling the group, "government is an industry of its own, with its own environment and peculiarities, much like any other industry, such as the entertainment, manufacturing, or transportation industries. Unlike the commercial sector in which accounting principles are established by the Financial Accounting Standards Board, or FASB, it is the Governmental Accounting Standards Board, or GASB, which sets accounting principles for public entities, such as state and local government, hospitals, and colleges and universities. FASB does, however, have jurisdiction for accounting in private hospitals, colleges and universities, and private nonprofit organizations."

One of the staff members asked, "How about the Feds?"

"Well," Paul laughed "God handles them. No, seriously, Federal law provides that the U.S. Comptroller General prescribes accounting principles for the Federal government."

"But," the enterprising staffer continued, "doesn't that create a sort of conflict? The Comptroller General sets Federal accounting principles and his agency, the GAO, is also the chief Federal audit agency, auditing for conformity to its own principles?"

Paul smiled and responded, "That's a topic for the advanced session, several weeks from now. But recently a Federal Accounting Standards Advisory Board was created to recommend accounting principles for the Federal government, using a due process similar to that employed by GASB and FASB. For now, remember that government, as an industry unto itself, has its own membership and professional organizations, such as the Government Finance Officers Association, the GFOA, and the Association of Government Accountants, the AGA. They, in turn, have their own professional journals, the *Government Finance Review* and *The Government Accountants Journal* respectively, among others. If you want to keep up with developments in this industry, you'll need to read these and similar publications. Remember too, this sector has many characteristics that set it apart from other industries. For example, the great concern for accountability in the use of public funds leads to use of the fund concept. We'll return to this in detail."

"In the absence of a profit measure, we all spend a lot of effort searching for new ways to measure performance in the government and nonprofit arena—hence the notion of GASB's movement toward calling for more reporting of service efforts and accomplishments. Performance auditing is also a natural outcome of the lack of net income for many government programs."

"Also, there is much more attention given to budgets and budgeting, and to comparisons of actual results to budget. Further, because sources of revenue are less direct and immediate, that is tax revenues, for example, and not sales revenue, there is less attention to measuring costs and cost accounting. Ask a public university official to break out the costs for you of a particular program and watch the looks you get. On the other hand, probably due to pressure of third-party payers, such as insurance companies and the Federal government, all hospitals, including public ones, have generally had strong cost accounting systems. Historically, there has been less attention in government to internal controls, but this is improving as the *Yellow Book* and auditing standards call for greater attention to internal controls, and even, a written report by the auditor on the entity's internal control structure and assessment of control risk. Indeed, it is fair to say, in most important aspects, governmental accounting and auditing are changing rapidly, and for the better."

Paul continued, "One environmental matter that has historically been a real problem for CPA firms is the matter of media coverage and access to information. Many of you know that in private-sector work we don't typically deal with the media, and they don't seem to bother with us, except in unusual situations. However, it's not the same in governmental work. Auditing standards generally call for widespread dissemination of audit reports. Relevant Federal and state laws make many meetings open to the public and media. And, though various state courts are handling the issue differently, we must assume even working papers are eventually available for all to inspect. And the media always seems fascinated by aspects—make that negative aspects—of government audits. But this situation will not go away, and we need to learn to deal with the media appropriately."

"OK," Paul concluded. " See you next time, and we'll move on to some details of specific accounting principles." Paul followed his students as they left the room, nearly walking into Tom Spivey who was waiting for him in the hall.

7

When Tom Spivey told Paul about the death of Stefie Hamilton, their sorrow, like that of most of the partners and staff of Dodney, Harrison, was deep and genuine. She had been a nice young woman with a promising career in the firm. Paul said he only hoped that the Washington police would somehow locate the madman, probably a drunken madman at that, who had run Stefie down. What a terrible, terrible tragedy.

At a hastily called meeting of the twenty partners in the Cleveland headquarters, they had decided how to handle the personal aspects of Stephanie's death—condolences to her parents, representation at the funeral, and so on. At that same meeting the partners' attention had quickly turned back to business—to be precise, Stephanie Hamilton's work in Washington on behalf of the firm. To be even more precise, how was Dodney,

Harrison to complete the audit of the White House staff, and do so in the most economical manner possible? And, of course, "How" quickly becomes "Who" in the public accounting business.

Paul Sandler knew that indeed life—and business—must go on, and that the partners had to concern themselves promptly with such practical issues. They had a responsibility to the client who had hired them—and in this case a most influential client—as well as to the firm, its partners, and staff. And so, Paul had participated fully in this grisly meeting, registering his agreement with most decisions. Still, he could not completely ignore the questions and doubts that invariably follow tragedy—the meaning of existence, the fleeting and temporary nature of life, how quickly a breathing and vibrant human being is forgotten. Heavy, heavy thoughts for anyone, including a hard-headed public accountant with a list of eager and demanding clients.

This is what comes of being a damned social scientist, thought Paul Sandler. His undergraduate education had been in the liberal arts, with a focus on political science. After several years working a variety of dead-end jobs, he had decided to get some more specialized training, and so Paul had enrolled in night classes in business administration and accounting. To his surprise, he had done well, and easily passed the certified public accounting examination. He had then immediately joined the ranks of Dodney, Harrison and had become a partner at the age of forty. Despite his solid credentials, his colleagues still kidded him about his liberal arts roots. Like many of his co-workers in the firm, despite his enjoyment of what money could buy, including providing for himself and his family, he still cared a great deal about what he did to earn his generous salary.

At forty-eight, Paul Sandler had most of the joys and sorrows of a man in his forties. His hair was thinning. He was ample (not fat) and constantly fighting a battle with calories. He loved tennis and played an enthusiastic if not totally skillful game, as often as he could. One of Paul's great curses in life was the fact that he suffered from severe tennis elbow. And there was never enough time to practice and play his beloved tuba. Yes, tuba. Even though he was genuinely good at it, it offered another obvious target for further ribbing by his colleagues.

Paul deeply loved his wife and family, and his position as a partner with Dodney, Harrison allowed him to take good care of his family. He and his wife, Allison, had met as undergraduates, and they had married upon graduation. Children, however, had not come for several years. The arrival of three children, the first two in fairly quick succession had been the key motivation behind Paul's decision to become an accountant. He needed a good job. Allie, Paul, and the children now lived in a small, fashionable community south of Cleveland, known as a haven for executives from both Cleveland and Akron. With the oldest daughter and son in college, and just the youngest daughter still at home,

Paul and Allie had recently sensed their lives changing still again and their house seemed to get bigger as the children spent less and less time there.

Paul occupied a large, attractive window office, and since Dodney, Harrison's offices were on the seventeenth floor, he had a good view of both the city and Lake Erie. Great for work and planning, as well as for contemplation, or daydreaming. Now, gazing out of the window, deep unsolvable problems occupied his thoughts. But in his business, he had learned long ago that such moments of reflection could not last very long. There was a light knock on Paul's door.

"Paul, may I come in? I need to chat with you again for a few minutes," Tom Spivey asked, leaning in the door. Tom had always had a such a relaxed, professional manner. The two had come to be pretty good friends.

"Sure, Tom, c'mon in," Paul responded.

"Stefie's death has hit us all hard, Paul. She'll be missed. Since she has worked under your supervision as much as that of any other partner, I know it will affect you a lot," Tom began.

"Funny, Tom, what doesn't get said at our meetings. Stefie kept her personal business out of the office. I may be one of the few people in the firm who knew she was about to announce her engagement. I've met the guy. Do I call him, or what?" Paul asked, as he turned back to window.

"This has caught us all by surprise, Paul, to say the least. None of us know how to respond, or what's appropriate. We shouldn't forget Stephanie. At our next partners' meeting I expect we'll establish a scholarship in her name at her alma mater, Kent State University," Tom offered.

"That's a nice thought, Tom, and maybe the best we can do. Let's be sure our legal people stay in contact with the Washington police. I want to see that S.O.B. caught."

After a pause, Paul added, "Should I call him, Tom?"

"Call who, Paul?"

"Stefie's fiancé."

"No, Paul, I'm sure her parents have already taken care of that. But it would be nice for you to talk to Stephanie's parents. Others have already called, but it would still be nice."

The two men stood side-by-side, looking out the window, absorbed in their own thoughts. After a moment, Tom turned to Paul and spoke, "Paul, after our meeting this morning I talked further with some of the partners. We're in agreement that it would be in everyone's best interests to finish the job in Washington as quickly as possible. I know it's unusual for a partner to play such an active on-site role, but we feel you should finish the work there yourself. Sending a partner would probably reassure the White House staff. Governmental and nonprofit accounting is your specialty. Although the progress reports suggest a few glitches were beginning to develop, Stefie was pretty far along on the job, so you shouldn't need to spend too much time in DC. How about it?"

Paul knew that the essence of the partnership concept was that each partner did what was needed to get the job done. But there were complications.

"What about the Columbus city audit? We just won that engagement, and I was to play a lead role. Also, I am at a critical point in our work with the Akron School District. Trying to interpret the financial statements to both the teachers' union and the school board to minimize friction during negotiations has turned out to be very tricky. However, if we pull it off, it could become a specialty area for us and lead to a lot of work."

Tom thought for a moment then responded, "We'll work it out. We'll try to delay a bit, and shuffle some of the work to others. Right now, the DC job must come first."

"One other problem, a personal one. This means I'll have to be away a lot, and Allie will be really teed off. I just told her I would be close to home for some time now. And Jennifer has some important high school events coming up. I wouldn't want to miss them, and I'd catch it if I did."

"Paul, Washington is an hour away by air. You'll

need only a few weeks to finish the job. You'll be home every weekend, and you could come home during the week if you had to."

"OK," Paul agreed. "Count me in."

"Thanks, Paul. We'll all feel better now, knowing you'll give this your personal attention."

Lord, Paul thought, *that was easy. Now for the hard part.* He had two difficult phone calls to make. First, he needed to phone the Hamiltons. Then he would have to break the news of his new assignment to Allie.

8

The Hamiltons, while genuinely appreciative of Paul's call and sentiments, could barely talk. In fact, Mrs. Hamilton, in bed, could not talk and did not come to the phone. "Thank you, Mr. Sandler," Stephanie's father said. "Stephanie respected and liked you. Your call helps. She was a good kid, no, not a kid anymore. She hated that, when I said 'kid', but she was a nice, young lady. She... ."

Mr. Hamilton just stopped, unable to go on.

"I understand, Mr. Hamilton," Paul said by way of helping out. "She was a nice, young lady, and I believe I understand your loss. I have two daughters of my own, not really kids anymore either, and if this happened to one of them... well, I understand."

"She was worried, Mr. Sandler, and I didn't take it

seriously," he had added. "Stephanie didn't worry easily, but this work she was doing had her worried."

"I don't follow you, Mr. Hamilton. Worried about what? Was she concerned she could not get the engagement completed on time?" Paul asked.

"Well, yes, that too," he responded. "But it was more than that. One weekend, at dinner with us, she told us that crowd in DC was giving her trouble. Seems they were trying to convince her to ignore some information she was pursuing. I sort of sided with them, since it didn't seem like a big deal to me. She wasn't too happy with me either."

After expressing his sincere condolences, Paul said good-bye. He really did understand Mr. Hamilton's pain and loss, insofar as anyone could when someone else's child died—or was killed. A horrible waste. So senseless. *They've just got to catch whoever did this*, Paul thought for the tenth time that day.

Unlike his first call, telling Allie had been far easier than Paul had anticipated. Of course, he had emphasized the one-hour flying time between Cleveland and Washington as well as the critical and sad nature of the assignment. Allie's acquiescence, it turned out, was heavily influenced by her own busy schedule. She had just completed her own course of study in accounting with a focus on taxes, and was actively seeking clients.

"Things are moving fast, Allie, faster than I'd like.

I'll need to leave for Washington tomorrow, but before I do, I have to meet with the Akron people on my school district engagement. So I'll need to hurry off to that meeting early in the morning and then go back through town straight to Cleveland Hopkins Airport. Sorry."

"I'll miss you, Paul, but I wasn't going to have much time for you anyway. In fact, I was going to ask you to cook dinner most nights," Allie laughed.

"Thanks, Hon, it's nice to feel missed. Will the kids also be all broken up?" Paul asked jokingly.

"Christina and Stephen are quite involved at college anyway and won't be home for a few weeks. Jennifer has a new boyfriend and doesn't remember she has a family. If you schedule a bawling out each weekend, that ought to take care of her needs," Allie offered.

Jennifer, at sixteen, was the epitome of all the joys and disasters of a teenage girl.

After agreeing to talk over the details of Paul's absence when he arrived home that evening, Paul and Allie said good-bye, and Paul made a third and final call—to the airport to arrange his flight to Washington.

9

John Barlow sat at his desk staring at the various reports spread out before him. Still, nothing was making much sense. He couldn't understand what Pete had found that made him such a threat that he had to be murdered. Pete always let him know when he discovered something big. But Barlow had heard nothing from him since he had left. Either Pete was about to uncover something or had actually found something and just neglected to call this time. Barlow put his head in his hands and sighed. It was difficult to think like a reporter when his friend's death was involved. John knew one thing though, he was going to find out why Peter Wilson died and tell the world. John also wanted to do the same for the young auditor who had died. "The whole thing is an outrage," he bristled to himself, between grief and anger.

Barlow wanted to go to Phoenix himself. He paused to think, his assistant could run the paper, but his family was going to be more difficult, if not impossible, to rearrange. He couldn't just have an assistant father-to-be step in for him while he was gone. His wife was due to have their first baby any day. They had both waited so long for this, and he didn't want to miss the delivery. Because both he and his wife were in their forties, the delivery might be more complicated. Barlow groaned, his head ached with the gravity of his decision. He needed to stay in Washington, but the guilt of his friend's death weighed heavily upon him. He felt personally responsible and wanted to give this investigation all his attention. "I'll just have to work something out and quickly," Barlow told himself.

He picked up the phone to call his wife Libby. While explaining to her all that had happened, John heard a loud voice call, "Barlow!" John quickly told Libby he'd call her back, hung up the phone, and began to head for his office door. But before he could get there, it opened and in walked Roberta Glover.

"Great. You're still here. John, I was worried that you might have left for Phoenix. Since you haven't, I want in. Whatever you are doing about Wilson's death, I want to be included. I just heard about his so-called accident two hours ago. I figured if you paid for Peter to fly to Phoenix, it must be a big story. I dropped everything and came directly here."

Roberta Glover was a freelance reporter who was

both a stand-in poker player and long-time friend to Peter and John.

"Great to see you Roberta. The bad news is, I don't know what I am doing about Pete's death," John replied. "I think I should go to Phoenix, but Libby is due any time now. I've been sitting here for the last couple of hours trying to go over these reports and trying to arrange how I can get to Phoenix. I am thinking of calling Libby's parents... "

"Stop," Roberta interrupted. "Why do you need to go, if I am going? You know I was as much Peter's friend as you were. You also know I am a good reporter who specializes in sleazy deals like this. Why would I want to drag an aging editor and worried father-to-be to Phoenix with me? You would be a big weight around the ankle. Listen, I'll get to the bottom of this and write a great series for *The Globe* — at my usual rate, of course. So, tell me, what story was Peter developing?"

John smiled. As long as he had known Roberta, she had always been abrupt. But he knew she meant well, and she was a great free lance reporter. If he could afford it, he would employ her full time, but *The Globe* could never afford her nor would Roberta be happy reporting only in Washington.

Barlow knew that the topic of the story would incense Roberta Glover further. "This started as a story about financial irregularities at the White House."

Glover got animated. “I would love to dig up some dirt on the White House and really shake things up. We haven’t had a decent president since Alexander Rose was assassinated by those terrorists. President Jonathan Rose is just a puppet of his sister, that old witch Marian Rose.“

“Oh, Roberta.”

“Furthermore, his predecessor, Dave Huggard, was no better. In fact, I think Marian talked Alexander into selecting Dave Huggard as his running mate just because he was such a pliable wimp. When Huggard became president after the assassination, I swear that he asked Marian for permission to go to the bathroom.”

“Roberta, is that second hand or did you hear him ask?” Barlow baited.

Glover ignored him and continued, “When Jonathan Rose got elected, the people thought that they were getting another Alexander Rose. Unfortunately, all they got was a Huggard clone.”

“I love unbiased reporters,” chuckled Barlow.

“Oh really. Listen, I know for a fact that Alexander Rose was going to eject Marian from the White House and take away all of her authority. She was really panicked. In a sense, those terrorists saved her ice cold butt and kept her as the Oval Office power broker — her and that weasel, Frank Norman. I even tried to find a link between Marian and the terrorists, but there was none.

Marian Rose keeping her job as the White House Rasputin was just a consequence that made the assassination doubly unfortunate."

"Okay, I agree that their father, Senator Samuel Rose, must look down from heaven and wonder what it is that he spawned," replied Barlow.

"Samuel Rose wasn't exactly perfect. He was a racist, sexist pig that became a multi-millionaire on a Senator's salary," countered Glover, "so I don't think it's a sure thing that he was heavenbound."

Barlow sighed, "Let's get back to the assignment. Roberta, you're hired for this story and, of course, I'll authorize travel to Phoenix — as long as you promise to be careful. Pete was investigating some strange White House expenditures and may have been killed because of what he found. This situation has gotten even uglier. This morning I found out that a young Cleveland CPA who was managing an independent audit of the White House was questioning the same strange Phoenix bills that Pete was investigating. She also met with a fatal accident. Now you and I know the odds of that happening. And I just received an encrypted email message from my White House source saying that the audit that started this whole mess is conveniently being canceled. So someone in authority is seriously worried about what this audit has been uncovering. That means the odds of a third person having an 'accident' from investigating these same activities are extremely high, so... "

"So," interrupted Roberta, "knowing the odds of the game before you enter makes one a more astute player. I know the rules, John. You and Pete taught me poker well."

John shook his head and mumbled, "Great time to be flippant, Roberta—I'm serious. Something dangerous is happening in Phoenix, and it's stupid to be over-confident if you're going out there on an investigation for this newspaper."

Roberta looked down at her brown hiking boots. "Well," she said, "if you're done preaching, why don't you tell me everything that's happened so far so I can go to Phoenix as well-informed as possible. Then I will very cautiously find out what's going on and who killed Pete."

John glared angrily back at Roberta and said nothing.

Roberta's voice softened. "You know you have to stay here. You know I can handle an assignment like this. So let's get going. John, I hope you don't think Pete's death is your fault."

"But," whispered John, "I didn't properly warn him—I, I had no idea—and he didn't even want to go. I was just following up on a White House tip. You know with these kinds of assignments, you usually just end up waiting in some bureaucrat's office for hours."

Roberta's voice returned to being crisp, "I thought you might feel it was your fault. It's the murderer's fault. Now come on, you were a reporter once. Stories with great potential sometimes carry great risks. If Peter heard you just now, he would give you a lecture entitled 'Stupid'. I miss him too, but his death wasn't any more your fault than it was mine."

"You're right," agreed John. "With the baby coming and Pete's death I just feel a little overwhelmed. Okay. You go to Phoenix alone, but contact me every twelve hours. I'll carry my cellular at all times. If I haven't heard from you in twelve hours and five minutes, I am calling the police and getting on a plane to come after you myself. So don't forget! And if you find out anything, no matter how small, call me with the information. I want to know what's happening in Phoenix at all times."

Roberta smiled and sat down in the chair across from John's chipped wooden desk. "Agreed," she said. "Now tell me everything you told Peter before he left. Oh... but first we have to come up with a way of stopping the cancellation of that audit. We need to keep these guys under pressure, whoever they are."

"Good idea," said John. "Leave getting the audit back on track with me. I know a few pressure points myself. Now," barked John, "grab a pen and paper and pay close attention."

10

Now, settled in for his flight to Washington, Paul reflected on the strength of his 26-year marriage. He and Allie had been through a lot together. They could kid around and be pretty rough, but never forgot how very much they meant to one another. He thought often about the nation's deteriorating family values and hoped desperately his children would avoid the pitfalls that seem so prevalent.

He also thought about the morning's early meeting with the officials from both sides of the Akron School District wage negotiations, the teachers' association and the superintendent's office. Paul's job on this engagement was to help both sides agree on the district's financial position and condition. While on the surface this would appear to be an easy task, in fact, it was turning out to be very difficult. The fund concept, at the root of much of government and nonprofit accounting, made a lot of sense both historically and in current times. It made it easier to account for and ensure that monies were used as intended. For example, if a special tax or grant were approved to raise monies for a specified purpose, using a special revenue fund for accounting helped guarantee that the newly raised monies were not misused. The problem was that the Akron School District had dozens of special revenue funds and some of the teachers' representatives were convinced that they were being used to hide monies that might be legally used for salary and benefit increases. Paul was still trying to find a way to persuade the teachers that the school funds were being used appropriately. At least none of the State Auditor's reports over the past several years had disclosed any inappropriate accounting practices.

Because of the eleventh-hour arrangements of the Washington engagement, Paul had initially scheduled a flight from Cleveland to Washington, by way of Detroit—inconvenient, but the best he could manage at the last minute. Fortunately, 15 or 20 minutes before that flight was to leave, Paul was able to reschedule at the airport and board a direct flight to Washington. He barely had time to phone his office to inform his secretary about his flight change and ask her to phone Allie.

That phone call, as it happened, was a piece of luck that saved Allie, and others, a good deal of worry. When Paul was settled in his hotel in Washington that evening, he phoned Allie. It was their custom for Paul to phone her every night he was away. When Allie answered the phone, her voice was unusually subdued.

"Oh, Paul, I knew you were OK, but I am still so happy to hear your voice."

"What's the matter, Allie? What's going on?" Paul asked, worried and surprised by Allie's response.

Allie responded, "Paul, the flight to Detroit, the one you originally planned to take, has had a terrible accident. No one yet knows any details, but it doesn't look good. Thank God you changed flights. I hate your traveling."

"I'm OK, Allie. Please call the office first thing tomorrow and reassure them..." Paul began.

"I'll call Tom tonight. He's already called here."

"OK. Good. I'm OK, Allie, so stop worrying. Take care and I'll call tomorrow night. Tell Jennifer I love her. I love you. Bye."

"Good night, Paul. I love you too. You've hardly started and I already hate this assignment."

Me too, Paul thought as he hung up. Fortunately, he was a good sleeper—a "sack artist," as Allie put it. Despite the day's events, he fell asleep quickly. Still, he had time to tell himself as he drifted off to sleep: "Let's just finish this job and get home to Cleveland. There are bummer jobs and this is one of them."

11

Paul had tried very hard to phone the White House staff and inform them of his firm's plans for completing the audit. Unfortunately, he had no success getting through to anyone in authority and had ended up simply leaving several messages about his planned arrival.

He had some trouble even getting through building security, but that was eventually worked out. There were now no other firm staff members on-site, since they had been told to return to Cleveland for other work until Paul could fully assess the status of the engagement. After long and confused discussions with several secretaries and other staffers, a woman finally said the magic words: "Hello, Mr. Sandler. Mr. Norman will see you in thirty minutes. Mr. Frank Norman is a Special Assistant to the President. We were all so sorry about the death of Ms.... , Ms...."

Paul helped, “Ms. Stephanie Hamilton.”

“Yes,” she continued. “By the way, I’m Sarah Harding, Mr. Norman’s secretary. Let me show you the office you will be using while you are here.”

As Paul scanned the office that Ms. Harding directed him to, his feelings about the engagement were confirmed.

Yes, thought Paul, *a real bummer job. We put our trainees in far better space. Cleveland, here I come.*

Sarah Harding came for Paul a short time later and led him to Frank Norman’s office. The two men shook hands, and Paul stifled a moan as the handshake further aggravated his tennis elbow. Norman also expressed his regrets at the death of Stefie Hamilton. At least he remembered Stefie’s name. Then, obviously not wanting to waste time, he told the partner from Dodney, Harrison, rather directly, to go home.

“Mr. Sandler, I am very sorry you have wasted your time by coming here. We intended to get in touch with your firm after Ms. Hamilton’s death, but, frankly, it just slipped by us. Our circumstances are such that we no longer need this audit, and we have too much going on right now to spend time on it. Perhaps we’ll have the General Accounting Office, or someone else, finish the job within the next several months. Don’t misunderstand me, we are not unhappy with your firm. I’m sure we can work out a satisfactory arrangement concerning your fee.”

Paul's reactions were varied. He was surprised. He was secretly delighted from a personal viewpoint, but he also knew such an ending to the contract might be misinterpreted and damage his firm. As Paul assessed the repercussions of the engagement's conclusion, he was distracted by his sudden realization that there was another person in the room, a woman. She was watching from a chair in a far corner. She returned his gaze but said nothing.

"I'm very surprised and sorry to hear that, Mr. Norman. I hope this is not because of any misunderstanding with Ms. Hamilton. Before leaving Cleveland I did take the time to review some of the working papers she had sent to my office, and I understand that you believed she was, perhaps, overzealous in her determination to follow-up on the details of the audit. Even so, except for what appeared to be a few minor issues, the audit seemed to be going well," Paul began.

"No, no, " interrupted Norman. "Nothing like that. Ms. Hamilton seemed quite competent."

"In addition to Stefie's natural concerns about following auditing standards," Paul continued, "she was also undoubtedly influenced by the findings of the U.S. General Accounting Office in its review in the late 1980s of governmental audits by public accounting firms. Following congressional hearings and internal review by the American Institute of Certified Public Accountants, the profession agreed to some positive changes, in part to avoid governmental regulation. This regulation is currently the responsibility of the American Institute of CPAs and state boards of accountancy. Coverage of the government and nonprofit accounting field has become a larger part of the CPA exam. Also, the GAO's auditing standards now require that individuals performing governmental audits complete at least 80 hours of continuing education every two years, at least 24 hours of which must relate to government and governmental auditing. And there have been other changes, too. In any event, my firm was initially interested in this job because it seemed to be setting a fine precedent for other parts of the Federal government. While I've not yet had time to go over the records in great detail, my understanding is that we are close to being done. I also worry about appearances. I would like to change your mind if that is possible."

"No, I don't think so, Mr. Sandler. But we'll be certain to make it clear that your firm was doing a good job for us. You could use us as a reference with no difficulty," Norman responded.

Norman was about to continue when Sarah Harding knocked softly and put her head through the door. "Mr. Norman, John Barlow from *The Globe* is on the line and insists he speak to you now. What should I do?"

"I'll take it, Sarah. Thanks. Excuse me for a minute, Mr. Sandler," said Norman apologetically as he picked up his phone. "Hello, John. What's up?"

As Norman listened he became first puzzled and then

very angry. “How did you know about this? Who the hell is running to you people with this stuff?”

Apparently receiving no satisfaction from the individual from *The Globe*, Norman quickly recovered his composure and took a new course. “John, we’ve got a million things happening over here. We’ve simply changed our minds about this audit. It was our idea in the first place. It’s taking too much time and money. That’s all.”

After a moment, Norman responded, forcing himself to be genial, “I don’t know, John, maybe you’re right. Maybe canceling the audit would be misunderstood. Especially since you’re sure to write about it now. We’ll give it some more thought and let you know.”

Norman hung up, thought for a few minutes, and then turned to the woman still seated quietly in the corner. “You heard. What do you think?”

She rose and stepped forward a bit. “Hello, Mr. Sandler. I am Marian Rose, the President’s sister. I’ve been trying to help sort out this unhappy situation.”

Since they were still some distance apart, Paul merely said, “Hello.”

Marian Rose turned to Frank Norman and said in a low voice something which sounded like, “We’re stuck.”

Then Frank Norman made the decision, “I’m not

going to try to fool you, Paul. I want to cancel this audit, but some snitch has leaked that to the press. They'll make it look juicy and dirty. We can't afford that. Looks like your trip wasn't wasted after all. You can keep working unless my boss overrules me. Looks like what started as a nice gesture to promote good government management just bit us on the..."

They spent a few minutes on logistical items. As Paul left the office he heard Norman on the phone. "Sarah, get John Barlow over at *The Globe*."

Paul walked slowly back to the broom closet that passed for his office. Even a partner must get his workstation in order, so Paul set about the business of locating his supplies, figuring out how to use the phone, and asking logistical questions of anyone who would help. In short, he did the mundane things any wandering auditor or consultant must do if he or she is to be productive. Then he received his first phone call.

"Hello. Paul Sandler," he answered.

"Mr. Sandler," responded Sarah Harding, "Mr. Barlow at *The Globe* wants to talk to you. He is on line two."

Paul thanked Ms. Harding and switched to line two, "Hello, Mr. Barlow, this is Paul Sandler. How can I help you?"

Barlow quickly recited a series of suspicions about cover-ups, murders, and misused funds.

Paul tried to mask his puzzlement and frank disbelief with a professional response, “Mr. Barlow, my firm has a simple policy governing contacts with the media. We don’t have any. Let me explain why. Generally Accepted Auditing Standards forbid us from disclosing any confidential client information without the specific consent of the client. For this reason, as well as good business practice, all media contact must be handled through our client and, since you already know Frank Norman, that shouldn’t present any problem. Anyway, the audit isn’t done yet, so there is little to talk about at this time.”

“Mr. Sandler,” Barlow said, “I don’t give a damn about your audit. Something else is going on and somehow your audit is in the middle of it. My sources are sure of that. You start an audit and a young woman gets knocked off. I send a reporter, and friend, to Phoenix on a tip. He ends up drowned in a swimming pool with his car parked several blocks away. We need to talk.”

After they had made arrangements for a breakfast meeting the next day and ended their conversation, Paul thought, *What a mess*. And his Cleveland office, Allie, the kids, and his home, suddenly seemed very far away. He looked forward to his call home that night even more than usual.

12

Paul Sandler spent the balance of the afternoon doing two things: trying to figure out generally what was happening, and going through the working papers Stefie Hamilton had put together to document the work she had done.

Paul Sandler had little luck sorting out the day's events. The audit is on. An auditor dies. The audit is off. A reporter calls. Then the audit's on again. *I'm no detective,* mused Paul, *but certainly Norman's behavior is odd.* Still, while Stefie appeared to be having trouble getting some answers, she never once indicated to Paul that she had found anything extraordinary during her review. But John Barlow's allegations were troubling, even if he was the crackpot newspaperman Paul supposed him to be. Was the audit tied to a story his paper is working on, a story a reporter-friend of his died working on? Died working on. Just like Stefie.

With the shocking and chilling thought that perhaps, somehow, these events were linked, Paul turned to the several large binders before him, the working papers left by Stefie the day she died. The day she... He got that sinking feeling again. Paul was grateful, at this moment, for the field work standard requiring a detailed record of audit evidence in the form of working papers. Maybe he'd find some answers.

Even in the age of the computer, Paul's firm still had an iron-clad policy that significant work items used in the audit be printed out in hard copy. Analyses, interpretations, and notes related to the audit needed to be initialed and, with relevant computer copy, bound in files for the firm's records. Paul spent several hours meticulously reviewing the working papers to determine how much progress had been made and looking for any sign of something that was not right. All he found was the usual stuff—some inventory control problems, too many people ordering and buying supplies, some petty cash lying around.

The working papers indicated that Stephanie Hamilton was close to completing the audit when she died. As he had taught her when she began working for him, she had prepared a short listing of the several items remaining to be completed. The list read:

Locate two missing PCs

Are procedures authorizing travel written down anywhere?

Those lousy roses!!

"Roses? Roses?" mused Paul. "Not just roses, but 'Those lousy roses!!'" Was this a complaint about the presidential family?

That item stood out. The others were the usual items this type of audit might raise inquiries about. Someone took a piece of equipment to work at home, or moved it to another office. Variations in approving travel, or the absence of such approvals, raised questions about the need for and existence of a formal written policy. But roses? Still, Stefie was good. She knew her stuff, and she was thorough. Paul remembered one time on an audit she had... *Enough flashbacks*, he thought and shook his head. Her sampling procedures uncovered some flower purchase which she still had to track down, he concluded. With that he continued on through the files.

Then, as Paul Sandler had feared, he found confirmation, although he still wasn't sure of what. It was in the third and fifth volumes under the headings, "Sample of Monthly Transactions." A page was missing in each volume. Paul knew that no accountant with Stefie's training and experience would remove pages out of the working papers. She just wouldn't do it. So, where were they? And, what was on them?

Paul Sandler reached for the phone and called his office in Cleveland. Ann Sharpley, his secretary, seemed genuinely happy to hear from him. "Mr. Sandler, we all knew you were OK. Allie called us. But it's still nice to hear your voice."

"Thanks, Ann." His secretary's reference to the downed aircraft had reminded him of still another strange occurrence. The thought that the plane crash might be related to this audit, to Stefie's death, chilled him.

"Ann," he continued in a dry voice, "you remember the progress reports and copies of working papers on this job? The ones Stefie Hamilton brought with her when she came back to Cleveland? They're in my office on the top shelf behind my desk. I only had time to review her periodic progress reports, but not the working papers. I need you to go to the working papers and get page 47 in volume three, and page 17 in volume five. Go ahead. I'll hold."

Paul knew what was coming. The details were not important. One or two keys would make the difference.

"Mr. Sandler, I have the working papers. Ms. Hamilton had included extensive appendices. The pages you mention are here. Each shows a whole series of transactions."

"Please read all the details to me, Ann, starting with volume three. It's very important."

After about five minutes of predictable transactions with no signals from Stefie, Paul heard what he'd been waiting for—several transactions in Stefie's sample were unusual. The dates, amounts, services, and other details were included. They were all for flowers, roses to be precise, and they were from a florist in Phoenix. The total was just over $5,000 and appeared to be for several months, maybe a whole year.

"Holy sh..." Paul stammered.

"I'm sorry, Mr. Sandler?" Ann asked, surprised by Paul's response.

"No, Ann, I'm sorry. Please copy those pages and fax them to me here. And put those records in a safe. And thanks, Ann. I'll be in touch. You know how to reach me if you need to."

As Paul hung up the phone, there was a soft knock on his office door. "Yes?" The door opened slowly and a very attractive woman, who appeared to be in her early thirties, entered.

"Mr. Sandler?" she asked.

"Yes, I'm Paul Sandler."

"I'm Denise Bartley. I work for Mr. Norman. I was asked to see if you have everything you need for your work."

The office Paul was using was so small and cluttered there was barely room for one person in it, let alone two.

There was a second chair, but he doubted anyone short of a super athlete would be able to weather the obstacles to make his (or her) way to it. Still, it seemed the polite thing to do. “That’s very kind of both of you. Would you care to sit down, Mrs. Bartley? I mean...”

“Ms. Bartley, or just Denise will do, Mr. Sandler.”

“I’m sorry, Ms. Bartley, but after all I am middle-aged and an accountant. Old habits die hard.”

“That’s quite all right, Mr. Sandler. And thank you, but I must move on. Do you need any supplies? Phone instructions? Equipment?”

“Thanks again,” responded Paul. “I am all set. Did you know Stefie Hamilton?”

Denise Bartley seemed genuinely sad as she responded, “Not really, Mr. Sandler. I saw her a few times as we passed in the halls, and we said ‘Hello.’ I never really spoke to her. She seemed to be quite professional and cordial. I’m very sorry. It was a terrible thing.”

“Thank you, Ms. Bartley. Do you know any of the details of her death?”

“I’m afraid I don’t. Of course we all saw the account in the newspapers, but that’s all. Most of us had very little contact with her.”

“May I ask, Ms. Bartley, if that were the case, why you are here now? Not that I don’t appreciate it. But I am curious. What little information I received from Stefie indicated she was having trouble getting anyone's attention."

Denise Bartley was clearly taken back by this apparent contradiction. "I don't know," she began. "I guess I am here because my boss asked me to be sure you were taken care of. I'm sorry if Ms. Hamilton was not treated well. Maybe it's because you are a partner with your firm and she wasn't. This is Washington, Mr. Sandler, and people pay a great deal of attention to rank."

He decided to let that comment drop, and asked, "Ms. Bartley, how long have you worked for Frank Norman? How often does he see the President? Do you ever deal with the President? And how long..." Paul stopped, embarrassed. "I'm sorry. I sound more like a reporter than an accountant. I didn't mean to sound so nosy."

"That's all right, Mr. Sandler. You just have a small dose of Potomac Fever. I've worked for Frank Norman since the early 1980s, ever since I met him when I came to Washington as an exchange student from a small college in the Midwest. At that time President Rose was Vice President in the Huggard Administration and Mr. Norman was a special assistant to the Vice President. Mr. Norman spoke to our class and I became totally caught up in the Washington scene. I never returned to my college, began as an intern in Mr. Norman's office, and finished college at George Washington University. Mr. Norman can see President Rose any time he thinks he needs to. Because I work directly for Mr. Norman I occasionally see the President, but it's not common. Let's see, does that about cover it?" She smiled.

"Thank you," Paul responded. "You've been very kind to an ol' midwestern boy."

"Let me know if you need anything, Mr. Sandler," she said as she began to leave. "Oh, yes, I almost forgot, Mr. Norman wants to meet you for dinner tonight if at all possible. He was thinking of 7:30 at your hotel. The restaurant there is called The Keys and is quite good. He could meet you in the lobby. Can I tell him that those arrangements are satisfactory?"

"That will be fine, Ms. Bartley."

After Denise Bartley closed the door behind her, Paul Sandler could only remark to himself, "Good Lord. Meetings with reporters and Special Assistants? What's next?"

13

Accountant and midwesterner that he was, Paul Sandler arrived in the lobby of his hotel at 7:20 p.m. and waited for Frank Norman to arrive. Promptly at 7:30, a flustered Denise Bartley walked up and greeted him. "I am so sorry, Mr. Sandler, but Mr. Norman was delayed. He asked that I meet you and we begin dinner without him. He will join us shortly."

"That sounds fine, Ms. Bartley," Paul responded. "Being in public accounting I am quite accustomed to such delays. It's nice to see you again."

Over salad, he learned more about this midwestern college girl who got caught up in, as she put it, "the Washington scene." From the work she described it was clear that, while her title was not impressive, her responsibilities were.

"Sounds like every young person's dream come true," commented Paul. "The perfect career. Surely there must be some downside to your work. There is to every job."

"The dragon lady," muttered Denise, rolling her eyes.

"Excuse me?"

Denise laughed and explained, "President Rose's sister, Marian, is a bit... , well, a pain in the neck. I know it's bad form to say such a thing, but everyone knows it anyway. Including the President. She is a devil to work for, and closer to President Rose than anyone, including Mr. Norman. The President seeks her advice on a lot of issues, and really listens to her. Her whole life has been tied up in her brothers' political careers, first Alexander Rose and then, when he was killed, Jonathan Rose. Although, from what I hear through the 'grape vine,' President Rose and his sister were beginning to disagree over things, just before he died."

Quite a dynasty, reflected Paul. From a very, very wealthy family, Alexander Rose had been elected the first time, and then reelected. Then about half-way through his second term, he died tragically as a result of a crazy assassination plot. His Vice President, David Huggard from Arizona, had completed his term and was then elected and reelected to his own terms of office. When he chose the dead President's brother, Jonathan, to be his running mate that first time, it was viewed as a brilliant political and strategic move. Huggard was a

Republican and westerner and needed the support of the more liberal Roses from the Buffalo area. As predicted, the move had brought New York and some of the other populous states along. And Jonathan Rose was well qualified, having served for a couple of terms in the Congress and in Alexander's administration as Attorney General for several years.

Paul added, "I had no idea she played so prominent a role. I've heard stories, but..."

At this point, a waiter approached Denise Bartley and told her she had a phone call. She left the table for no more than five minutes and, while she was gone, for the first time in this entire wild caper, Paul felt he knew what was happening. He was, therefore, not surprised when Denise returned, again flustered, and stated that Frank Norman was simply unable to join them. "Mr. Norman is terribly sorry he can not get away, and insists that dinner must, at least, be our treat. Apparently, some problem came up regarding a presidential trip."

What, gracefully, could he say? Paul mumbled something to the effect that he understood. He did, but not in the way he meant. They continued with what was a very good meal.

The small talk continued, now somewhat more strained on Paul's part. He was uncomfortable, embarrassed and fearful about what might occur next. His instincts were solid.

"Mr. Sandler, are you married?" Denise asked, smiling coyly.

"Yes, I am," Paul responded without meeting Denise's gaze.

"You strike me as a man who has been married for many years," Denise continued.

"I will take that as a compliment and as a comment on my character. I have been married long enough to have children who are almost, but not quite, your age," Paul remarked dryly.

Paul felt as if he was in a bad movie when Denise Bartley uttered the inevitable proposition, "Mr. Sandler, the reason I stayed in Washington ten years ago, and the reason it still thrills me, is the chance to be close to older men who do important things, wield great power." As she spoke, she placed her left hand on Paul's right hand, which was on the table.

Paul pulled his hand away and responded, "Ms. Bartley, I may be an accountant, and I may be from Cleveland, but I am not from the farm. At the risk of guessing wrong, but not a big risk, let's get a few things straight. I believe this conversation, make that this whole evening, is an assault on my professional integrity and on me personally. This may be a strange time to be citing standards from my profession, and I won't bore you with great detail, but, believe it or not, such situations are covered. For example, general auditing standards talk about the need for auditor independence, and freedom from both external and personal impairments that would keep us from doing our job right. Mr. Norman has tried the first by attempting to influence the scope of our audit or dictating audit procedures. Now you're trying the second by creating a personal relationship that might cause me to limit our inquiry or disclosure, or slant our audit findings. I'd like to add that you seem to be too nice a young lady to be involved in such a charade. What's this about anyway, testing my character, setting me up for blackmail? What?" Not really wanting an answer, he stood up, put his napkin down, and, turning to leave, remarked, "I agree, it should be your bill."

Denise was surprised by Paul's reaction, obviously not accustomed to it in her circles. To her credit, she also seemed embarrassed. She clearly did not know what to say.

Momentarily, Paul Sandler felt sorry for her, but his anger quickly returned and he walked away.

14

Despite his growing apprehension about this engagement, Paul had slept reasonably well. He awoke, well-rested, and dressed for his meeting with John Barlow.

When they had talked on the phone the day before, Paul had made it clear to *The Globe*'s managing editor that he could not discuss details of the engagement with him, at least not during the audit. Sure, the "sunshine laws" applied; that is, he must adhere to relevant laws regarding the eventual public access to information generated with public funds, but only when the audit was completed. And even then, court opinions varied as to the availability of working papers which supported the final audit report. "Besides," Paul had told Barlow, "I don't know anything you'd be interested in yet."

Nonetheless, here he was on his way to meet this paranoid *Globe* editor, who seemed to see something sinister around every corner. *A typical, ambitious news-type*, Paul thought as he headed for the restaurant. Paul realized his attitude towards the media reflected not only his own experiences with the press, but also his profession's biases. He had been persuaded to meet Barlow, only when Barlow had told him, "You listen, I'll talk. All I'm saying is if you know what I know—OK, suspect—then it may influence your audit work. Don't you feel it should?"

Paul had responded, without enthusiasm, "We'll see," and then proceeded to explain the restrictions imposed by the audit process regarding accumulating evidence and performing test work.

When they met, they exchanged pleasantries, ordered, and wasted no time sparring. "Look, Mr. Barlow, I'm not even supposed to be here. And I don't know you, so don't get out-of-joint if I don't seem to trust you. I'll listen, but I'm not saying a word."

"All the terrible things I ever heard about accountants are coming to life before my very eyes," Barlow interjected dramatically. "You want a clean audit, you want to get done, and you want to collect your fee. To hell with the country. Is that it?"

"Look, Barlow, I didn't want to come here for this very reason. God made accountants and newspaper people as one of his many inexplicable tricks on mankind. We distrust each other. We're *supposed* to distrust each other. The needs of the media conflict with auditing standards and the ethics of the accounting profession. They make us natural enemies."

"What are you talking about? I'm not after a one-hour course in accounting or auditing."

"Forget it. They must have put vodka in this tomato juice," Paul responded, unwilling to begin a debate with Barlow.

"No. Sounds like BS to me, but new BS. Go on."

Paul Sandler did not even want to be present, much less deliver (or hear) lectures, and he certainly did not want to debate the matter. He tried to state his opinion as succinctly as he could.

"Look, all I mean is this. You guys are not bound by any professional code, principles, or standards. There are no required educational qualifications and no certifying exams. If I do not follow the rules of my profession with regard to the proper conduct of an audit, not only could my permit to practice as a CPA be suspended or revoked by my state board of accounting, my firm could face some pretty serious liability problems. Among other things, you have few, if any, rules of evidence or documentation. What the hell is an 'unnamed source'? If you screw up you don't lose a license to practice. You leave someone gutted, but you just go do your damage elsewhere. An 'unnamed source' says... for

God's sake. I've dealt with you guys. A reporter rushes in, after the audit and says, 'Got anything good?' He means 'bad', of course. I give him a copy of the audit report and he says he's fighting a deadline and doesn't have the time to read it. So I offer him a summary of the audit and he says, 'Just give me a few zingers to write around.' Even if I try to straighten out the facts, it doesn't matter. The headline (yeah, I know, it's written by someone else) blares out whatever will sell a few more papers."

Paul stopped, embarrassed. That was succinct?

Barlow smiled. "Well, well, well, what have we here? You were either dumped by a female reporter once, were ignored by the media when you gave your valedictorian address in high school, or you've been mixing airplane glue with your accountant's ink. Sure we have some bad reporters, and sure we have many of the problems you suggest. But we also have a lot of good and decent reporters helping this country. But let me see if I have this right. A public accounting firm charges the government client a fair fee for its work, scrupulously follows all the accounting guidance from the authoritative bodies as it does the work, and fully completes the contracted work, even if the firm will lose money doing so. Oh, and if and when an accountant gets into trouble, his buddies will drive him out of the profession?"

Barlow was on a roll, and scoring points, so Paul Sandler interrupted, if a bit weakly, "I didn't say the accounting profession was perfect..."

"Perfect?" Barlow responded. "We have a public report by the U.S. General Accounting Office that basically says that on one-third of all government contracts, the accountants screwed up, and often badly. And, guess what, ol' buddy, the profession hasn't done jack about it. Those same guys, the ones doing bad work, are now selling their wares in other cities."

Paul was thinking that actually the last point wasn't true. The profession was making corrections to "clean up its act." But he decided that, while this might make for a great debate, it wasn't getting him very far here. And, he did have a meeting to attend soon.

"OK, OK," Paul said, "both fields have some problems. Maybe we can watch each other."

Barlow could not resist, but now commented in a very different, almost kindly manner, "Now you're talking like something more than just an accountant."

Both men smiled, even laughed a bit, and that helped.

"Look, Paul, I know this is hard on you. Your firm has lost a valued employee. You are trying to finish a job which the White House would rather forget, but can't. You'll soon be losing money which, I'm sure, won't please your partners back home. But I'm asking you to just consider that the stakes here might go beyond your firm's engagement alone. Sure, you could finish up, fudge a report, collect your fee, go back to Cleveland and not ruffle any feathers. But you're an American too, and what if something is going on? And I believe it is."

Barlow stopped. Paul thought for a time, and then asked, "But, John, do you have any evidence? I'm not a reporter. I'm not good at this. In fact, I have no right to go around just generally interrogating people. The principles which guide me here state that if monies may have been misused, then I should keep going. Field work standards state that in the case of errors, irregularities, and illegal acts, I may, with caution, extend my audit steps and procedures to get a better fix on what is going on. But I need to be very careful that I don't mess up some future investigation. Another option open to me is to terminate the audit if I judge that by excluding further audit work in some areas I cannot reach solid professional opinions and conclusions. I could also report concerns to some other body without proceeding. But I don't feel I am at that point yet."

"And have you discovered any irregularities?"

"As a matter of fact, there is not much information at this point. And," Paul continued, "where we have concerns, the amounts of money involved are very small."

"And does that mean that you cannot or should not continue to check into those items?"

"No," Paul responded, "We have a lot of discretion. In this case the amount of money is not the most important thing. At first glance, the expenditures seem to be for odd purchases, but it may turn out that they are for allowable activities. We will resolve all outstanding items. Again, professional guidance gives me quite a lot of discretion on how far to go to resolve my doubts."

"I received a tip about some unusual expenditures in Phoenix. My source doesn't know what's going on, but when the people he works for get too worried, then he worries. And right now, he is very worried. I sent a friend to Phoenix to check all this out and he's dead—a mysterious death at that."

There is another Phoenix connection, thought Paul.

Barlow stopped for a minute or two, and then plunged on.

"I've been in this city and this business a long time, Paul. Maybe too long. Something's not right. These could well be a string of unconnected coincidences, but I don't think so. And I don't believe you think so either. Dave Huggard was Vice President when President Rose was assassinated and so became President. Maybe this was even lucky. Next election he chose Alex Rose's little brother to be his vice presidential candidate. Now little brother is President. And big sister Marian has been in the wings, calling the shots, throughout. A tightly knit group of henchmen if there ever was such a group. In a weird sort of way, the death of Alexander Rose may even have worked to the benefit of Marian Rose and Frank Norman. Word has it that the President was unhappy with the role these two were playing in his administration."

"Your politics aren't showing, are they, John?"

"You're right, Paul. I'm a Democrat, and I don't like the politics of this gang. I won't lie to you. No point in it, since my position is clearly on record. And I don't much like them as people either. But that's not what this is about. Something bad is going on. That's why I want your firm to be the ones to sniff it out."

Paul thought a while. He decided to consider John Barlow's story and believe his motives. But that wasn't the point. He himself had the same nagging concerns. The problem was, he was an auditor, and this so-called "gang" was, in a sense, his client. What loyalties did he owe his client? Who truly was his client? Was his client, in some sense, really the taxpayers of the U.S.? Despite this issue of client loyalty, auditing standards offered ample guidance—the CPA firm must judge management integrity in accepting or retaining a client. Still, while Paul had his doubts, this was still THE White House. If this were a private firm, his decision would be simpler; but he had chosen governmental and nonprofit accounting as his specialty.

"I appreciate your concerns, John. A decent and talented young employee died trying to complete this engagement. My view right now is that auditing standards indicate we should continue with our work. My firm will continue to pursue these matters. And, while I can't be in continual contact with you, if you have any evidence of problems, please send me the details. I promise that when we finish and all this is public, you will be the first to know, but just a little ahead of others."

"That's good enough for me, Paul. That's all I ask."

The two men shook hands and parted, with a grudging respect for each other.

John Barlow didn't notice the nondescript station wagon that had been parked near the hotel when he left. When the driver saw Barlow get in a cab, he made a hasty trip to the White House.

When Paul returned to his room to pick up his briefcase and gather up a few items, he had a phone message. He called the front desk and was told that his Cleveland office had called. He was to drop everything and return there at once to meet with Sidney Harrison.

"OK," said Paul to himself. "Why not?"

15

With the audit back on track and with the CPA firm's engagement partner clued in to the whole story, John Barlow and Roberta Glover felt it was the perfect time for her to go to Phoenix. After promising again to call John anytime something new came up, as well as every twelve hours, Roberta boarded a plane to Phoenix.

Roberta knew she would have to be cautious, but believed she was in little danger because no one knew she had joined the investigation. Sure, she had done a few stories for *The Globe*, but she had done a few stories for almost all the big papers.

Roberta opened her briefcase and went through her notes. She planned to retrace Pete's footsteps in Phoenix as best she could — starting with the rental car agency Pete used. But first, she had the sad task of going to the police station to claim Pete's remains and to retrieve his belongings that were left in the car. She instinctively felt that she would have to be the most careful at the police station. The Phoenix police had ruled suspiciously quickly on Wilson's case, so she would need to be on the lookout for informants. It was all too likely the White House officials had "friends" in the Phoenix police force.

Roberta always felt that the truth went over better than a cover. So Roberta had called the Phoenix police and notified them that Peter Wilson had no family, and since she was a close friend, she would be picking up his belongings and would see to his burial. She would send his remains back to Washington where a memorial service was scheduled for friends.

She hoped to find some clue in Pete's belongings that would help bring her closer to some answers. She was determined not to leave Phoenix until she got what she came for — to find out who killed Peter Wilson and why.

Roberta shifted in her seat and wondered why she felt so uneasy about this assignment. *Why?* she thought to herself, *I've been on far more dangerous assignments.* But before she even allowed herself to finish that question, she knew that none of them had been so personal.

The intercom broke into her thoughts. "Ladies and gentlemen," said a sugary voice, "please prepare yourself for landing."

When she arrived at the airport, Roberta rented a maroon Dodge Intrepid.

16

"Hello. I'm Allie Sandler. How may I help you?"

The office manager in the small accounting firm where Allie worked had just phoned on the intercom about a new client who had specifically asked for her. Now she was escorting the man into Allie's office. A very nice sign, she thought, given the fact that she had only recently started her accounting career. Indeed, while Allie had not yet passed all parts of the CPA exam, she had passed three parts, including those which most related to taxation, her first love.

"Hello, Mrs. Sandler. It's a long, involved story that brings me here today, and I'll try to shorten it. I am in Cleveland on business from out West. I happen to know your husband and his firm. Actually, I should say I know of your husband and his firm, since I've never met Mr.

Sandler nor had any direct dealings with his firm. I'm Robert Parish."

With this he reached for a business card and handed it to Allie across her desk. It read, simply, "Robert Parish, Parish and Company," with a phone number and "Phoenix" written in.

Allie had grown accustomed to obtaining clients through Paul's contacts and gladly accepted such help. Paul's firm was short of staff in the tax field just now, and generally avoided taking all but the most affluent individuals as tax clients. For this reason Dodney, Harrison was, at least temporarily, referring some prospective clients elsewhere. And Allie was grateful. In this business, increasingly competitive, you learned to take whatever help you could get.

Allie's prospective client continued, "My small company is doing just fine, but Dodney, Harrison is a bit pricey for me. Also, I understand Mr. Sandler is not in the tax business. And that's where I need my help."

Even though her guest was dressed in a business suit, Allie noticed—anyone in Cleveland would have noticed—the western flair to his clothing that included a strikingly large turquoise ring.

"I'm delighted you're here, Mr. Parish. How do you know my husband and Dodney, Harrison?"

"As I say, Mrs. Sandler, I don't know either directly. I have friends back home who have had dealings with them."

Paul always said Allie had good instincts, and her instincts told her this man was not leveling with her.

"May I tell Paul who your friends are? He likes to keep on top of such things. It goes with this business."

"My friends are very influential people, Mrs. Sandler. The type of people who do not like to have their names bandied about. Just tell Mr. Sandler he has powerful contacts back in my home town. Tell him I am in Cleveland a lot. I can get here quickly. And I keep up with his practice. For example, I even know he is in Washington right now working on a very delicate government engagement. I have been asked to help him, and tell him to be very careful, to listen to the advice of friends."

Allie didn't need any special instincts to realize this was a warning, or a threat. She was not certain what to say, or whether she should say anything.

"I'll return to discuss my business, Mrs. Sandler, when you have more time. As I say, I can get here anytime I want or need to. Here's a couple more cards. Please give one to your husband, and one to your daughter." With this he handed Allie two more business cards, and turned to leave before Allie could say a word.

17

Paul was determined to complete one additional scheduled item in Washington before he returned to Cleveland to see the big boss. He had planned to attend the National Intergovernmental Audit Forum quarterly meeting, which was to be held this time at the headquarters of the GAO. The National Audit Forum in Washington brought together accounting and auditing representatives of the Federal agencies, state and local government audit organizations, and CPA firms to discuss and try to resolve common problems. There was also a series of regional audit forums which met frequently in various parts of the country. Paul had come to realize that regular attendance at these meetings was a great way to keep up with current professional developments and meet the top executives and officials who attended the meetings. And, of course, it helped keep his firm's name before officials. He would attend the meeting and still be able to return to Cleveland that day.

Today's meeting agenda had listed progress reports and informational presentations on several items important to Paul and to Dodney, Harrison, both for current practice and for preparing for the future. As the meeting progressed, Paul could see he would not be disappointed. First of all, attendance was very good. Every chair around the very large combined tables in the GAO meeting room was filled, and an overflow crowd sat around the perimeter. Between 75 and 100 individuals must have been present.

The current chairperson, Elaine Hoby, was a high-ranking official from the Office of Management and Budget, or OMB, in the Executive Office of the President. She began by reminding those present that a revised draft of the *Yellow Book* was now being distributed throughout the country, and that the comment deadline was approaching. She asked for members' cooperation in providing constructive critique on a timely basis. Some good-natured joking took place when Sam Atkins, the City Auditor of Austin, remarked, "Are you saying, Elaine, that you folks in Washington, DC, really need the advice of folks way out in Texas?"

To which the Chairwoman responded, amid laughter, "Sam, those of us in our nation's capital realize that good ideas can come from many sources, even some pretty strange ones. I assure you I will personally scrutinize your comments on the proposed revision to the *Yellow Book*."

Elaine Hoby then asked the Legislative Auditor of Kansas to introduce the next topic on the agenda—contracted, substandard audit work by CPA firms. Paul could feel the tension rise in the room. Over the past few decades the volume of governmental audit work was growing rapidly. Because of the enormous growth of Federal programs and expenditures during the 1960s and 1970s, some estimates placed the number of Federal grant audits at well over 50,000, up more than five-fold from the 1950s. Federal grants-in-aid to state and local governments grew from $2.2 billion in 1950 to over $100 billion in 1990. In an effort to reduce the number of audits while improving continuity and audit coverage, the Federal Single Audit Act was passed in 1984. Under the terms of this Act, each state and local government that receives Federal financial assistance of $100,000 or more in a fiscal year is required to have an audit conducted under the terms of the Act and OMB Circular A-128. Under the Act, over 19,000 governmental units were required to have annual audits. While state and local government auditors conducted some of this work, they relied heavily upon CPA firms to perform audit services as well.

John Williams, the Kansas Legislative Auditor, began, "As you know, my committee has been serving as a liaison with others in the profession who continue to be very concerned about this matter. Through the regular processes, various State Boards of Accounting have disciplined some CPAs already, and that process continues even now. In response to concerns about a lack of adequate training of auditors, the American Institute of CPAs is now offering a series of continuing education opportunities throughout the U.S. Some of us have participated in these sessions either as presenters or members of the audience. Also, recognize that coverage of governmental accounting has been becoming a larger and larger part of the CPA exam and that currently about a third of one of the half-day sessions is in our field. That's about the same coverage as managerial accounting and taxation. The bottom line is we've had some problems, but we're working on them. And we must continue to do so, since a few congressional committees are watching the process closely. As you know, the U.S. Congress has passed the legal responsibility for regulation of the accounting profession to the Securities and Exchange Commission. The SEC, in turn, is leaving it to the profession to police itself. The National Association of State Boards of Accountancy, and the State Boards of Accountancy, which are the entities with the legal power to supervise the profession, buttressed by the AICPA, our professional representation group, handle the regulation for us. But we, as individuals and professionals, need to stay on top of this. Please pass on to me or other committee members any ideas you might have on this issue. I think you can sense how important it is."

"John," interjected Elaine Hoby, "perhaps you had better remind us all of the names of the other committee members."

"Stan Paxton from San Jose, Glenda Petrie from Maryland, Ralph Bledsoe from the Federal Department of Housing and Urban Development, and Kirsten Marley from Deloitte Touche," was the response.

Paul left the meeting at about 2:30 p.m. in order to get to the airport. Lunch had been brought in at noon and, after a brief recess, the meeting had resumed. It was still continuing when Paul slipped away to catch his flight, but he sensed it was winding down. Much of the balance of the discussion was taken up with two items—a progress report on GASB accounting pronouncements, especially as they would impact the audit community, and a presentation of cooperative or shared audits in which governmental auditors and CPA firm representatives were working together. The theory was that such joint efforts would bring cost savings and unique expertise to the audits.

As Paul hurried down the hallway toward the entrance and, he hoped, a waiting taxi, he heard someone call his name.

"Paul, hold on a minute."

Paul turned to face Jason Trumble, the appointed State Auditor of Wisconsin. Paul had gotten to know Jason when, several years earlier, he was an assistant state auditor in the office of the Ohio State Auditor. The Ohio State Auditor was an elected position, but currently fewer than half of the states have elected auditors, the balance being appointed, usually by the state legislature.

Jason had made the change from an assistant in an elected auditor's office to the head, appointed auditor in another state.

"I'll only take a few minutes, Paul," Jason began. "I can see you are in a rush. But I want to see if you are willing to be on a committee we are starting, and which I am chairing."

"What's the committee about?"

"There is growing concern," Jason continued, "that attempts are increasingly being made by legislatures to curtail the independence of state and local auditors, especially the appointed variety. Sometimes it's real or threatened budget cuts or staff reductions, efforts to carefully circumscribe the scope of audits, attempts to change or even eliminate the term of office of the head auditor. You name it. It's happening. We think we need a couple of private practitioners on the committee to give us perspective. Also, politicians are more likely to listen to you."

"Let's see if I have this right," Paul said slowly, with a touch of humor. "You want me to put my name, and that of my firm, on a public report which will likely tell heavy-weight politicians to keep their mitts off the audit function, because it is in their best interest and good for them. Right?"

"Paul, you always did have a knack for getting right to the heart of the matter, which is why we need you on this committee."

"You'll appreciate why I need a little time to think it over, perhaps discuss it in my firm, and get back to you?"

"That's all I ask, Paul."

"Sure it is," Paul smiled as he again headed for the door.

18

Jenny Sandler didn't like it when her father traveled. First of all, she just missed having him around. When she thought her mother was too tough on her, sometimes he would intercede. One good thing about his absence, however, was that it freed up one of the two family cars so she could drive to and from school. This was especially convenient now that she was so busy. Classes all day. School activities nearly every day after classes. Family chores and homework each night. This high school junior year was turning out to be too frenzied for her. Unlike her sister and brother, she seemed to need a lot more time to herself. Time to just relax. Today, for example, when she would rather have headed straight for home, she had to stop at a mall to do some shopping for a friend's birthday. She liked shopping, and Missy was a good friend, but still, she did have a lot of homework waiting for her.

She drove into the mall parking lot, choosing a spot close to Jay's Books. Surely she could find a suitable gift for Missy here—something she could afford, and something she could find in a reasonable period of time. If not, a couple of nice clothing stores were nearby. She headed straight for the bookstore.

Missy was a big science fiction fan, so Jenny began to browse in that section. Not that she knew much about this stuff. Two school friends went by calling out, "Hi Jenny," as she continued to browse the shelves.

"This is too much to believe," exclaimed a man who had been standing next to her.

"Excuse me?" Jenny responded politely, unsure whether this man, dressed like a country singer, was startled at something in a book or had been speaking to her.

"Are you Jennifer Sandler, Allie Sandler's daughter?"

"Yes, I am. Do you know my mother?"

"Well, sort of. I just met her this morning. She may do some tax work for me. Actually, I know your father too. Your mother told me she had a daughter in school in this neighborhood."

"But how did you know... ?"

"Psychic," laughed the man. "I'm sorry. It's not very mysterious. Your mother and I were sharing family photos, and I just heard one of your friends..."

"Call me 'Jenny,'" Jenny concluded.

"I'm sorry I startled you. My name is Robert Parish. And, as a perceptive young lady like you could guess, I'm not from Cleveland. I am from Arizona. Phoenix."

Math was not Jenny's best subject. In fact, unlike her older sister, she didn't like any of her subjects all that much. Still, she realized that meeting this man here, in this way, at this time, must merit entry into a statistical book of records. Perhaps she had inherited some of her mother's instincts about people. She decided to distance herself from this man. Missy's gift could wait.

"It was nice meeting you Mr...."

"Parish."

"Before you leave, Jennifer," he said as he touched her arm as though to stop her, "be sure to tell your mother and father I said hello. Tell them it's nice they have such a charming daughter. Tell them to take good care of you."

As Jenny turned to walk towards the door, he leaned close to her, adding, "Jennifer, you shouldn't read this sci-fi trash." He held up a copy of the book which he had been leafing through, flashing a large turquoise ring on his right hand. "Too often in those books, nice young people come to tragic and horrible ends."

19

For Allie the rest of the day was like a bad dream, one from which she could not awaken. She struggled through the day, doing only that work she had to complete to honor contractual commitments.

Initially she wondered whether she had simply misunderstood her strange visitor. She very badly wanted to believe this. Not likely, she decided. He was certainly not a client looking for professional advice. He was there to scare her, or Paul, or perhaps both of them. Something about this crazy assignment Paul was working on in Washington. Paul had phoned yesterday at the office, saying he was coming home later that day. Some urgent matter at the office. He was having some trouble getting a flight on such short notice but would be home soon. *Thank God for that, anyway*, Allie thought.

But now she was home and feeling more secure. She was putting together a nice big chef salad which would take care of dinner for her and Jenny and stay fresh until Paul got home. Of course, he hated salads, but would say, "Oh well, at least it will help me keep my boyish figure." It was approaching six and getting dark already, as it did at this time of the year in Cleveland.

"Hi, Mom," Jenny said as she came through the garage door and gave her mother a kiss on the cheek.

"Hi, Jenny. You're a bit late tonight. I thought I'd come home and find you vacuuming, remember?"

"Oh yeah. I forgot. I stopped by the mall to buy Missy a birthday present. I'll vacuum tomorrow."

"And?"

"What?"

"What did you get Missy for her birthday?"

"Nothing. I was about to buy her a science fiction thriller at Jay's—you know what a nut she is about that stuff—when some guy you know comes up and starts talking weird. He really scared the devil out of me, Mom, but now I think I..."

Allie turned from the salad she was working on, asking, "Guy, what guy? Where? What did he say?"

"At the bookstore. He was weird, for sure, and I was scared, but I hope I didn't insult a family friend or mess up some business deal. It's just..."

"Jenny. Tell me everything."

And Jenny did. An out-and-out threat, concluded Allie. Her thoughts raced: *He came here all the way from Phoenix to seek me out. Let me know he could reach me. And... Jenny. The creepy no good... Something about Paul's work. Do I call the police, or what? Paul, where are you?*

The ring of the phone brought Allie's thoughts back.

Jenny was now sitting at the kitchen table, absorbing the fact that this man had also visited her mother earlier that day and that they—the whole Sandler family—were in some kind of real danger.

"Hello. Allie Sandler speaking."

"Mrs. Sandler."

"Yes?" Allie shivered. It was him.

"Mrs. Sandler. Believe me. I am at a phone very close to your house. I can be there in a few minutes."

Allie thought frantically. *A car phone? Right outside the house?* Anger overcame wisdom. "Listen, you creep..."

Jenny was now on her feet, eyes wide. "Mom?"

"Mrs. Sandler. Now, above all else, you need to keep your wits. That doesn't include name-calling."

"What do you want?" Allie asked firmly, trying to control her anger.

Jenny was beginning to panic, "Mom? Mom?"

"Let's get down to business. Before I lose my temper and do something we will all regret. We've established a few important things today. I can reach you at any time. I can also reach your daughter. Incidentally, I know you have a son and another daughter in college. I know where. I even know their dormitory room numbers. I can also reach them. I know workplaces, schools, and I know your home. As I said, I am very close right now. I know a great deal. But here is something you need to know. These very influential friends of mine out West want you to know this. I want you to know it. It is crucial you understand it. Your husband and his firm must stop their work on the Washington, DC, project. Now. And they must make it appear that there are no problems. That everything is fine. Communicate that to your husband. No, press it on him. Do I make our position clear, Mrs. Sandler? We'll be watching. We'll know. We will expect to see Mr. Sandler's firm wind up its work within the week."

It was clear that he was finished and about to hang up. But he did not hang up immediately because Allie had started to respond at once. She had been thinking. She knew what she had to say. Again, her essentially strong character overcame discretion.

"Listen, Mr. Parish. I don't know what rock you or

your friends have slithered out from under, but here are the Sandlers' thoughts on the matter. If you are smart enough to comprehend a bit of honesty and decency..."

Before Allie could say more, she heard a click on the other end of the phone as Parish hung up.

Jenny had been listening to the conversation with a rising sense of panic that was finally uncontrollable. Inexplicably she bolted, not upstairs, and not toward her mother, but out the kitchen door to the garage, where she had left the overhead door open when she drove in earlier.

In quick succession, Allie shouted after her, "Jenny!" and started for the door.

Almost simultaneously, Jenny screamed out, overwhelmed with terror, "No! No! Let me go! Let me go!"

Allie stopped, uncertain what to do. Phone the police? Go into the garage?

At that moment, the small side door between the house and garage began to open again. Allie froze in place.

As the door swung open, Paul entered, holding Jenny, who was sobbing uncontrollably.

20

It took them some time to calm Jenny, a task made more difficult by Paul's many questions. Finally, when Jenny had quieted down and gone to bed, Allie told Paul the complete story.

Paul shook his head and scolded, "Allie, that temper of yours could have gotten you both hurt or even, even..." He hugged her, unable to finish his thought.

"Killed?" Allie added. "Paul, who are these people, and what are you working on that could be so important to them? I don't understand."

"Allie, I don't know. I only know that since the audit of the White House staff began, there has been a long series of terrible tragedies. At first I thought it was just bad luck. Then, coincidence. Now I know better. I am involved in something so volatile that the people behind it are willing to go to any lengths to keep it quiet."

"But what could it possibly be?"

"I only have a few pieces. Stefie Hamilton was almost finished with the audit when she died, but a few of her concerns were not yet answered."

Paul shook his head, "She was probably murdered. She had a few loose ends, things an auditor can put on hold while finishing the more important test work, but can't ignore forever. It's a small amount of money by most standards, certainly wouldn't pass any usual materiality test. I mean, what's $5,000 on an operating statement showing over $40 million in expenditures? But it was chosen in Stefie's sample, and she was obligated to pursue it. Also, it may involve possible misuse of public monies for nongovernmental or personal purposes. She had to raise questions. So, it's a legal issue, and Stefie was thorough. She was investigating this when she... when she died."

"But what was the money used for?" Allie asked.

"Well, this is hard to believe, but it seems like someone was having a lot of roses delivered to Phoenix, Arizona. I don't know just yet. I was about to get on it when I received a message from Sidney Harrison to meet with him in the office tomorrow."

"Phoenix?" Allie added. "That's where Robert Parish, or whatever his name is, says he's from. Paul, why does the firm guru want to see you? You said he hardly even comes to the office any more. Is it about this audit?"

"I'm not sure, Allie, but I wouldn't be surprised. It just keeps getting weirder and weirder."

Paul continued, "There are other things too, although they aren't a part of the audit and therefore aren't exactly my concern. But they make me wonder. I've been contacted by a DC newspaperman. Seems someone in the White House has been leaking information to him about other odd, maybe illegal payments for things in Phoenix. It's possible that our audit made someone nervous enough to leak this stuff. The newspaper sent a reporter to investigate, and he turned up dead too."

"My God," muttered Allie.

"Funny thing," Paul went on, "it's a matter of overkill, no pun intended. They, whoever 'they' are, didn't need to do all this. For Stefie's sake, and the firm's, I had decided to finish the audit fast and be done with it. At one point, I might have even overlooked those blasted roses. They are an infinitesimal part of the expenditures of the White House. But then, when so many people tried to intimidate me, I decided I had to do the whole job. And now..."

"And now?" Allie asked.

"Now it's over," Paul responded. "It's too damned much to ask."

"Don't swear, Paul."

Paul always found it amusing that this woman who, when angered, could let loose with a string of expletives that would make a sailor blush, was constantly telling him to watch his language.

Paul continued, "Lord knows how many people have already been hurt by this, or died because of it. Nothing is worth that. I've got to back off."

"But that's not what you thought when you came home tonight, Paul. You were going to track down all the loose ends." Allie pressed him, "What has happened to change your mind?"

"You know damn well what's happened, Allie—and don't tell me not to swear. I am not about to get my family wiped out for the good of Dodney, Harrison and my career."

"But you were prepared to continue before, when you knew you were in danger."

"That's different."

Allie was both pleased with this middle-aged lummox, and also very angry. She was quiet for a few minutes, thinking. Then she began, no finished, because it was clear that her statements were intended to be final. No going back. No changing her mind. And, if Paul didn't agree, he was in big trouble.

"I think the kids and I are lucky to have you, Paul.

Someone who would sell out his principles to protect us..."

"C'mon, Allie, that's a low blow."

"Listen, Paul. I mean it. I know you, and I know how important it is to you to do the right thing. So, I know how much you must care for us. I didn't marry a CPA, a partner in a public accounting firm. I married a guy with a political science degree who wanted to make government better. I was proud of you when you turned down chances in your firm to do audits of large corporations and companies and, instead, did government and nonprofit work for less money. You even had to convince many in the firm that this was a legitimate area of practice for the firm. That's the guy I married. An idealist. An optimist. Not a quitter, and not a man who gives up and lets the bad guys win."

Allie stood up, indicating this conversation was ending. "Tomorrow I will begin a vacation, and Christina, Stephen, and Jenny will go with me. There are things more important than school, or work. We'll be safe. I'm afraid Paul, for us, and for you, but you need to do everything you can to make this one right for all our sakes."

21

Miraculously, Paul and Allie slept reasonably well that night. It seemed to them that if the "cowboy"—the nickname they had given Robert Parish—had intended any immediate harm, they would have heard from him earlier. And they had a very good security system. They did discuss going to the police, but decided against it. They agreed that they wouldn't believe this yarn themselves if they weren't living through it, and they had little proof of anything.

At about 3 a.m. they were awakened by the phone.

"Paul Sandler speaking."

"Paul, this is John Barlow in Washington. I'm sorry to phone so late, but I just got a call from a woman named Denise Bartley. Apparently, she works in the White House and knows you. Got my name from a mutual friend. I had a lot of trouble locating you."

"Yes, I know Denise Bartley."

Allie was sitting up. "Who's Denise Bartley?"

John Barlow continued, "I don't know whether she was drunk or overwhelmed with remorse. She says she had dinner with you and made a complete fool of herself. Says she was forced into it."

Half asleep, Paul responded, "Yes, I had dinner with her."

Allie was now fully awake. "So, who's Denise Bartley?"

"Anyway, Paul, she wants to let you know she's sorry. Says she got in over her head at the White House. She doesn't really know the details, but says be careful. You are in the middle of a big mess. Everyone, and she stresses everyone, is damned worried about this audit."

"John, tell her I appreciate the information and her concern. I..."

As though talking to herself, Allie asked, "Let's see, do I know someone named Denise Bartley with whom my husband dines?"

"Shhhh," Paul whispered to Allie.

"Excuse me, Paul?"

"Not you, John."

"Well," Barlow went on, "she doesn't want me to contact her, so I can't pass on any message. Her real reason for calling, though, was to give you some information. She thinks you are one of the few good guys left around and believes you'll do the right thing. She says you need to talk to a physician in Phoenix. He was Alexander Rose's personal physician until the assassination, and he is still connected to the Rose family. He was also tight with Dave Huggard when he was President. I guess he's wealthy, but still has a very small, selective practice."

"But John," Paul asked, "what right do I have to go up to this guy and start asking questions? He has nothing to do with my firm's audit."

"Paul, I've been doing my own research into governmental accounting. There have likely been other illegal payments out of government funds. Your roses are just a part of it. As an auditor, you have every right to track down all leads and even expand your sample. All you need is the will to move ahead."

Paul thought for a moment or two. "Good research, John. What's this doctor's name?"

"Dr. Alfred Holstein."

The minute he hung up, Paul realized he was in trouble, and not from Washington or Phoenix. From much closer to home.

"Denise Bartley. Denise Bartley. You know, I've

wracked my brain but don't remember anyone by that name. Could you enlighten me, please?"

"Look, Allie, it was business. It's late, and it's a very long and complex story."

"What kind of business? Besides, it's not late, it's very early, only 3 a.m. And I have a lot of time. As for the complexity of your tale, give me a chance to see if I can absorb it all."

This could be a long night, mused Paul before he began, "Well, I was having dinner with a Special Assistant to the President, a man, and this woman."

"This woman being Denise Bartley?"

"Yes."

"So, there were three of you at dinner then?"

"Not exactly."

"Is this where it gets complex, Paul, deciding whether there were two or three at dinner? If it is going to get much tougher than this, I'll go and get my calculator."

Paul first watched Allie, not fully understanding what was going on. Then, when she laughed, he began to laugh too.

Then he told her the entire story.

22

I*t's going to be a long day*, Paul thought as he drove toward his office in downtown Cleveland. They had been up very late and they had to wake early so Allie could contact her office, call Christina and Stephen, explain things to Jenny, and make all the necessary arrangements. Christina and Stephen would drive home that same day. Paul would take them all to the airport late in the day, and they would fly to Clearwater, Florida, where they would stay with Allie's mother until it was safe. Whenever that might be. This arrangement would leave Paul free to do what he needed to in order to complete this audit, and watch out for himself without worrying about Allie and the kids. He planned to return to Washington that very day to get the audit moving again.

Wheeling his car into his assigned parking spot

below the office building occupied by Dodney, Harrison gave Paul a feeling of comfort and security. A bit like coming home. At least it was still reserved for him. A good sign in these troubled days. He walked to the elevator and rode to the firm's offices on the seventeenth floor.

As he stepped off the elevator, Paul noted once again with pride the attractiveness of his firm's offices—the firm's classy sign, plush carpeting behind the large glass and brass-trimmed entrance doors, and the ample wood-trimmed reception desk within. Following procedure, he stopped at the receptionist's desk to let her know his plans for the day. A temporary, he observed.

"Oh yes, Mr. Sandler, we were expecting you. Mr. Harrison is already in and asked that you come to his office as soon as you can get settled. My name is Joan Richards. I'm from a temporary service. Apparently your regular receptionist is taking some vacation."

"Thank you. I need to spend a few minutes in my office before I see Mr. Harrison. If I get any calls, or you need me, my secretary will take messages or find me."

He walked to the end of a hallway, exchanging greetings with several younger staffers who shared the pleasant but smaller offices in the middle of the firm's space. As on any normal day, many of the staff members were out on engagements, attending meetings with clients to discuss tax and other matters, doing the actual audit or consulting work at the clients' locations, or attending continuing education sessions. Dodney, Harrison employed about 200 professionals, roughly one-half of whom were a part of the audit practice. The remaining half was about equally divided between the tax and consulting practices. The firm worked hard at maintaining its ratio of one partner per each ten employees. Most partners devoted all their time to a single practice area. A few, like Paul, split their time between consulting and auditing. In Paul's case, this was due to the fact that his main area of interest, government and nonprofit, while growing nicely, was still too small a portion of the firm's business to justify a full-time commitment to either auditing or consulting. But that, with luck and hard work, would change. Indeed, as with most CPA firms, the government and nonprofit accounting was a growing part of the business. Only a decade ago, indeed, even today, some firms would not do such work. They felt it was unprofitable. Further, they were concerned about the inevitable politics and media coverage. However, due to fierce competition, firms were learning to handle the unique environment of government accounting and to make money as well, in part by using appropriately trained personnel. In short, they were beginning to appreciate government accounting as a unique industry in which, with care, they could provide a service and make money.

Paul was relieved to observe that all the partners' offices were dark. He would not have to answer the inevitable "How's it going, Paul?" As partners, they had every right to ask, and receive an answer, but what could he say? "It's going fine, except that my life and the lives of my family have been threatened. Also, a couple of people, including Stefie Hamilton, may have been murdered. And we're likely to lose money on the engagement. See you later." That might create a bit of a stir.

A light was on in Tom Spivey's office and his door was open. As both head of the firm's audit practice and a friend, Paul did not know what to say to him. It looked as though Tom was reviewing the working papers and report on an engagement before signing off on behalf of the firm. As with most firms, at least two partners would normally review staff work. Engagements containing especially thorny issues might call for review by still other partners with specialized skills. Despite such care, problems still occasionally arose, as demonstrated by the litigation against CPA firms in the commercial market. Paul stuck his head in the door.

"Hi, Tom, what's my share of that job going to be? Got a tuition payment coming due."

"Paul, how are you doing? I heard you'd be in today. I was afraid by now you'd be so into the Washington scene you'd never return. Except maybe to run for Congress."

"Fat chance. You know me better than that. How are things here?"

"Good, Paul. We are doing just fine, considering we are in a bit of a lull. The government-nonprofit stuff is helping smooth out the peaks and valleys. The good thing about your area is that the need for the work often runs on a cycle which differs from much of our other work. Many private companies are on a calendar year basis, whereas the fiscal year for some public entities ends at other times. Any new projects in sight?"

"I'm always working on it, good buddy."

And he really was, as was every partner in his or her own area.

"Seriously, Paul, will this DC thing lead to more work? I'm already looking for space for a Dodney, Harrison office in Washington, DC."

If he only knew, thought Paul. Paul could only hope that at the end of this engagement there might still be a Sandler family, a government practice, and a firm.

"Tom? What's so important that Sidney would call me all the way back from Washington?"

"Paul, you know Ol' Sidney. He's like the 700-pound gorilla. Comes, goes, and does whatever he wants. Doesn't bring other people in unless it pleases him. In other words, I have no idea. Knowing Sidney, it could be as big as a new $5 million piece of work in New York City or the Department of Defense, or as small as a recommendation for a restaurant in Washington, or maybe he wants you to go to some special place to get seafood shipped back to Cleveland for him."

"Well, I'd better get in there to see what's on his mind. I'll talk with you later, Tom, before I head back. By the way, when I realized I had to be here today I asked that my training session be reset for this afternoon. Could they get everyone together on such short notice?"

"I believe so," Tom responded. "The training room was free, and all but one or two staff members were available. You ought to have a group of eight or ten. Professor Peabody agreed to do his part at a future session."

"Thanks for the help, Tom. See you later."

He was still unsure how much to tell Tom about either the tricky professional or personal problems associated with this engagement. Well, he'd see what Sidney had on his mind first, and then he'd decide.

He chatted with his secretary, Ann Sharpley, for a few minutes. In reality she was secretary to several partners. He brought her up-to-date on his plans (at least as far as he knew what they were). He also told her Allie would be away for a while, so not to worry if she couldn't reach her. Next, he collected some phone messages, told Ann how to deal with a few of them and placed the rest in his brief case. One message was from the Akron School District. He would want to call his contact there to see what was developing. Then he scanned some progress reports and other projects assembled on his desk for his review. Immersed as he was in this

Washington work, it was difficult for him to remember, much less devote time to, the several other projects currently under his supervision. One of the most difficult aspects of the upper ranks in public accounting was the need to learn to successfully work on several complex engagements simultaneously. Paul also placed these reports in his briefcase for reading on a plane or in his hotel room in the evening. Finally, he headed for Sidney Harrison's office.

Unlike the other partners, the surviving founding partner had his own secretary. Several of them often wondered what she did all day, since Sidney was in the office so infrequently. Some speculated her real job was to monitor his investments and schedule his social events.

"Hi Dorothy. Mr. Harrison is expecting me, I believe."

"Yes he is, Mr. Sandler. He has someone with him, but told me to let him know when you arrived." She buzzed the inner office, told Sidney Harrison of Paul's arrival, and then hung up.

Within a minute or two the office door opened and another partner walked by. Paul and Jerry Winston exchanged greetings. Jerry was building a very nice practice in the small business area, especially in working with entrepreneurial types. Paul continued into the office.

"C'mon in, Paul. Good to see you. I appreciate your returning to Cleveland on such short notice. Have a seat."

Paul sat down and waited. Sidney Harrison's office was impressive, like a scene from a movie. An old one, at that—no PC here, no signs of a high-tech society, just flat, plain old money, leather, wood and a beautiful view. The way a public accounting or law office is supposed to look. Business gets done here, but not work. And Sidney Harrison fit the role perfectly. He was elderly, but trim and fit. He had to be 70, well beyond the mandatory retirement age of 62 for partners, but since he founded the firm and wrote the rules, he could stay as long as he could walk through the door. *Sort of like a senior member of Congress*, Paul mused.

"You know me pretty well, Paul, and you know I didn't create Dodney, Harrison by talking in circles. You're in trouble, and that means we're in trouble. And, of all places, with the White House. You know I go back a long way with several people well placed in the last couple of administrations, and my phone has been ringing off the hook, day and night. What's going on?"

Paul dug in his heels, defensive, and hating the feeling that he was a guilty man trying to prove his innocence. "With all these phone calls by well-placed people, Mr. Harrison, I'm sure one of them volunteered the full story."

"Look, Paul, I know I'm getting old and that some of

you younger guys think I'm losing it. And to a degree I am. You will too. But I'm not senile yet. I've heard their side of the story many times. You're on a fishing expedition. A witch hunt. You've got it in for them. One person said you don't like their politics. Another said you're holding them responsible for that young woman's death. And..."

"Stephanie Hamilton. The young woman's name was Stephanie Hamilton."

"Yes. Well, you get the idea. All I said was I would talk it over with you. Talk to me, Paul. Tell me your side of all this. I talk too much, but I'm not a bad listener. I understand being a good listener is in these days."

"You know me pretty well too, Mr. Harrison. You hired me. You helped make me a partner. You said you didn't understand these government people or the government environment, but there was business there and, if the firm was going to go after that business, it had to do it right. You hired me because you felt I would do it right. And I am."

"Paul, I know you're capable. That's not the issue. I'm not worried about the technical stuff. But an auditor can't be involved personally. That's just as important. Are you? One caller said you were looking into such a level of detail, you'd trip up Ghandi. What's that all about?"

Before Paul could respond, Sidney Harrison lowered

his voice and added a few more sentences, revealing to Paul a glimpse of a man he had never seen before, or at least not for a long time. Perhaps he would never again see this side of Sidney Harrison.

"Paul, I believe in this firm and what it stands for. Like the world as a whole, about half of public accounting is bull. But the other half makes it all worthwhile. It's beautiful. I really believe in all the words we toss around every day. Words like independence, objectivity, professionalism. I believe we are a key part of keeping free enterprise and democratic government on the up and up. To keep it together. To keep it running. We're only a part of it, but an important part."

Then the elderly man looked Paul straight in the eye. Paul could feel the strength of his character, the steel in his backbone.

"Talk to me, Paul. Level with me. If you do, and you persuade me you're right, I'll back you all the way. If you don't, then you're all alone and dead in the water. We're on the same side, Paul. Bring me in."

Now Paul remembered why he'd liked this man many years ago, when he persuaded Paul to "do good" as he had put it, but from a different vantage point. Do good, he had said, as an insider, in a large CPA firm. He had liked and trusted Sidney Harrison then, and he liked him now, and would trust him.

So, Paul did level with him. He explained, "Sure a

few thousand dollars for roses wasn't a lot of money, but that's not the issue. It is a matter of..."

Mr. Harrison had interrupted, "... government auditing standards, possible misuse of funds, broadening the review. Materiality is not the sole issue in pursuing a potential irregularity. Because irregularities are intentional, they have implications beyond their direct monetary effect. I follow."

Good, thought Paul. *This guy still knows his stuff.*

"Don't be so surprised, Paul. Just like you, I still need to keep up if I want to keep my permit to practice. Go on."

"Yes," Paul continued. "It is personal. My family has been threatened. I have reason to believe that Stephanie Hamilton's death was no accident. And an editor from *The Globe* has contacted me with a number of other serious allegations against the administration. But the real issue here, Mr. Harrison, is this: Am I, are we, going to be driven off this engagement?"

"I want to know, Paul, about these threats and what kind of danger you and your family are in."

Paul provided the details.

After Sidney Harrison heard this account, he asked, "Shouldn't we walk away from this now, Paul? Turn it over to the authorities? I don't feel right about exposing you and your family like this. I want these people as much as you do, but no firm can ask someone to take such a risk."

"Mr. Harrison, we have no proof. I am probably a few working days away from nailing down what we need. I'll need to go to Phoenix, and they'll fight us every step of the way. But if we walk away, I'll feel that we lost something that we should have fought to win."

Sidney Harrison thought. Not about whether the firm should continue with the audit. He knew it should. He also knew the White House couldn't fire them. Too much explaining to do. Too many people knew now. But what is the "right" thing in this case? He couldn't allow his firm, his profession, to be scared off. Besides, someone was obviously hiding something that needed to be found out. But was it "right" to expose still more people to danger? If he had not been an idealist himself, the solution would have been simple—walk away.

"Governor Jones is an old friend of mine. He often says that Washington hasn't been the same since Alexander Rose was assassinated. The Governor has never liked Marian Rose and claims that Alexander was going to kick her out of the White House, but died before he found the right opportunity. He also claims that it was after the assassination when Marian Rose started gaining influence and when other troubling incidents began to occur. I guess he is right." Sidney Harrison paused for a moment, struggling with his own thoughts, and then quickly and firmly, he made his decision.

"I'm behind you," he stated firmly, "but I'm very worried, Paul, about you and your family. Let's move ahead, but please be careful. Keep in touch. Let me know how we can help."

Paul was touched and said so. He was also pleased to have Sidney Harrison's backing, especially since he would have gone ahead anyway, one way or the other.

"I'm sending my family away. If I did not believe they would be safe, I would never agree to go on."

"Good. Paul? What would you have done if I had decided we couldn't go forward in the face of such opposition? If I had taken you off the engagement?"

Paul hesitated, not wanting to lie or offend this man he respected so much.

"I thought so. That's why I hired you, made you a partner, and want to keep you healthy."

He shook Paul's hand, and they said good-bye.

23

Paul stepped into the classroom and prepared to begin the training session. He had rescheduled the session before he knew about Parish's threats, so he had to struggle now to clear his head of his problems which seemed to be growing rapidly.

Smiling at the waiting trainees, he started the session, "I usually do this session with some help from one or two professors, but they'll catch up with you next time. In the meantime, let's get started. The key to governmental accounting and auditing, particularly at the state and local levels, is an appreciation of the fund concept. GASB defines a fund as a fiscal and accounting entity with a self-balancing set of accounts."

"Mr. Sandler?" asked one of the staff members. "Previously we discussed the concept of 'entity' as it relates to, say, the city as a whole. We talked about what is supposed to be in and out of the entity according to GASB criteria. You said that accountability and oversight, as it pertains to resources, budgets, and key personnel, are key criteria for determining whether or not a bridge or hospital is included in the 'entity.' But is this a different definition of entity you're discussing today?"

"That's right," responded Paul. " Indeed, too much preoccupation with funds as entities can detract from focusing on the city as an entity: its finances, performance, and so on. So we must reconcile the two concepts. The GASB Codification provides sufficient detail to help us sort out what is part of the primary government entity, and the form of reporting for the primary government and the component units."

"Now let's focus on funds. The governmental funds include the general fund, any special revenue funds, capital project funds, and debt service funds. Then there are the proprietary, or commercial-like funds, both the enterprise and internal service funds. Water department activities, with outside customers offer the classic example of an enterprise fund, while the municipal garage servicing other city departments, illustrates an internal service fund. Remember, too, the two account groups, where fixed assets and long-term debt are recorded. And then we have a whole series of various kinds of fiduciary or trust-type funds. 'Fiduciary.' I like that word. Right out of Mary Poppins and old England," Paul mused aloud before continuing his lecture.

"It is a good old American tradition to be distrustful of government and, after all, we are accounting for public funds here. So, we record the transactions for the different kinds of dollars, or 'eggs,' in different funds, or 'baskets.' Then we watch the 'baskets' like crazy. For example, if a special tax revenue is to be used for a special purpose, it will be recorded in a special revenue fund. If a private donor provides resources to be used for specific purposes, transactions relating to the use of these funds will be recorded in some kind of trust fund."

At this point Paul displayed a series of overheads on a screen which illustrated sample accounting transactions for the various types of funds and account groups.

He then concluded, holding up a city's Comprehensive Annual Financial Report, "We end up with a report, or CAFR document, as thick as this one. And this is for the city of Kent, Ohio, a pretty small city! Does our preoccupation with funds cause us to create a CAFR which is so detailed and complex that we lose sight of the city? Some people think so, and that is why GASB is currently researching report presentations that combine some of these funds. Further, GASB and the Government Finance Officers Association are encouraging forms of 'popular reports' that are more useful to a larger audience. However, thus far there is not a lot of official guidance for popular reporting."

Paul placed the report on the table in front of him and continued, "Another important piece of research GASB has underway relates to the basis of accounting measurement. As some of you know, state and local governments currently use modified accrual accounting, which is an interesting blend of full-accrual accounting and cash-basis accounting. The first is used in commercial accounting, and the latter is a traditional basis of government accounting. For this reason, I suppose, proprietary funds use accrual accounting, while governmental funds use a curious mixture of a cash-basis recognition of revenues, as in the sales tax, and accrual recognition, as in the property tax. No great surprise then that depreciation is recorded in proprietary funds, but not in governmental funds. GASB is currently struggling with this and my guess is we'll move much closer to a full-accrual model within a few years."

"Recognize too," Paul continued, "that the closer we move toward fuller, clearer disclosure, the more politically unpopular such reporting practices are in some circles. Every time a liability previously unrecognized, or not fully recognized, is more clearly included in the CAFR, the smaller that Fund Balance is going to appear on the balance sheet."

"Politics," interjected one participant. "I thought this was accounting. What does politics have to do with it?"

"Generally accepted accounting principles," Paul reminded the group, "means just that. Generally accepted. Not law. Not unanimous. Not always popular. And this goes for FASB as well as GASB. Private companies bring the same kinds of pressure to bear on accounting reporting principles relating to pension benefits, including medical benefits for retirees, and to other areas which might make company finances look worse. Well, that's all for today," Paul finished. "Next time, your guest lecturer will take a closer look at all these issues with you. Any questions?"

A staff member spoke up. "Mr. Sandler, I was embarrassed a few days ago when one of our government clients asked me what we were doing on SEA. I faked it and said we'll be looking at that soon. What is it?" Laughter was heard around the room.

"I always save the best for last, Carl. And I'll be telling you more about SEA than you want to know. For now, you need to know a few things. First, it is not a disease. SEA means service efforts and accomplishments; in other words, what resources go in and what results come out. In this case, results mean efficiency and genuine accomplishments toward stated goals. Second, while traditional accounting data are a key part of SEA measures, the measures rely on other data too, with the result that the measures are really quite unconventional, at least for accountants. But we must learn and change. For example, we try to measure efficiency as the relationship of inputs and outputs, and effectiveness in terms of what goals were achieved. An example of an efficiency measure might be cost per passenger on a mass-transit system. A measure of effectiveness might be the percentage of buses or trains arriving as scheduled. The third thing you need to know is that we do a fair amount of work in this field already, whether in the form of performance or operational audits, or in the form of management reviews. We are always seeking ways to measure and then improve program performance. Lastly, GASB is very carefully researching this field and has already issued some preliminary pronouncements on it. While GASB is currently calling for more research and experimentation, my guess is we will have some reporting requirements within five to ten years."

"But," suggested Carl, "I'm not sure that's even accounting."

"It may be strange to us now," commented Paul, "but it will soon be an accepted part of accounting. Remember, too, that management accountants in private companies are also paying more and more attention to performance measurement, performance standards, including competitive benchmarking, and continuous improvement. See the similarity? But more on SEA later."

With this Paul dismissed the group, and his mind returned to his Washington engagement.

24

Paul had decided that, with the complete backing of Sidney Harrison, he did not need to plead his case nor provide all the gory details to Tom Spivey. The fewer people involved, he believed, the better. For one thing, it could be dangerous for Tom to know too much. So, following the afternoon training session, Paul briefed Tom on the status of the engagement, gave him some feel for how they were doing against budget (not good) and estimated completion of the work at an additional one to two weeks. He did warn Tom that the client was not pleased with the firm's thoroughness (tough, Tom had ventured), and that it could get messy.

"Define messy, Paul."

"Messy as in the White House staff, maybe as high as the Oval Office, has misused public monies."

"Are you telling me I should cancel the lease for office space in Washington?"

"I'm saying, Dodney, Harrison may give new meaning to the phrase, 'Take time along the way to smell the roses.'"

"Paul?"

"Yes, Tom?"

"A man's got to do what a man's got to do."

"Tom?"

"Yes, Paul."

"Shove it. I'm going back to Iwo Jima."

25

Before leaving the office, Paul called Allie to learn about her flight arrangements. He then scheduled his own flight to leave shortly after his family would leave for Clearwater. To get a flight at this late date, he had to purchase a first-class fare, which always annoyed him. As a partner, he was free to fly first class if he chose, but his habit was to avoid doing so to set, as he put it, a good example for the younger staff members. He had once computed the difference between a coach and first-class ticket to a given city and decided that the "free" drink, somewhat better dinner, and slightly larger seating space cost several hundred dollars. A fellow partner had jokingly told him they never should have hired a liberal arts-political science graduate, who then became a CPA.

As he left the office, he stopped by the reception desk to leave word of his plans. Joan Richards seemed like a very pleasant woman. She told Paul he had a few more phone messages, none urgent, and handed him the messages which he added to his brief case. She then said, matter-of-factly, that she had one more message. She leaned across the desk, and said in a somber voice, "Mr. Sandler, I was asked to come here today for the sole purpose of reminding you of the importance of your present project. You should end it. I know nothing about this project, but I know a great deal about my employers. They are very serious people who mean what they say. And they say you should walk away from this project. My presence here today is an indication of the power they have. Please listen to them."

With that she gathered up her few belongings and walked out, leaving the switchboard lit up and unattended.

26

The Sandlers were somber and silent on their way to the airport. That evening, around dinner time, Allie and Paul had agreed to pull few punches. They told their three children most of the story, eliminating only the details which, in their judgment, would frighten them unnecessarily. The kids knew they were in real danger because of an assignment their father was involved in and that they needed to be very careful.

Paul planned to leave his car in long-term parking. He dropped his family at their departure gate, had a valet help them with the bags, drove his car to the parking garage, and took the shuttle back to meet them. They said their good-byes, and Paul promised to keep them posted daily, and visit them if his engagement went on for much longer.

"I love you, Allie. Take care of yourself and our brood," Paul said warmly and then added, "I'm so sorry I got you into this mess."

"Never mind that, Paul," Allie responded. "We're in it now. Let's finish it up in style and fast."

He cautioned the kids, "Watch out for each other, and take care of your mother. Tell Grandma 'Hi' for me. Tell her not to bother saving any of her great Polish cooking; let Stephen finish it off." It was a family joke and they all smiled weakly at Paul and waved as they boarded the plane.

When their flight had departed, Paul sat down to wait for his flight. Too preoccupied to read the materials in his briefcase, he simply thought, and looked around. He only had 45 minutes or so to wait—*thank goodness the plane was on time*, he reflected—and then he boarded his plane for Washington.

The sad good-byes and worried departures of the Sandler family had not gone unobserved. In fact, two other individuals had watched the departure of Allie and the kids from a distance and with great interest. They also watched, discreet and unnoticed, as Paul boarded a plane bound for Washington. The observers were not together, and did not know each other. When Paul boarded the plane, each walked slowly to a phone to report on the destinations of the Sandler family. One observer phoned a special number at the White House. The second phoned Sidney Harrison at his home in a

Cleveland suburb. Then they left for their cars.

And then Paul Sandler, getting better and better at this new role of auditor-sleuth, left the aircraft bound for Washington, walked to another concourse and boarded a flight to Phoenix.

27

Allie stood on her mother's front porch. She paced impatiently for a few moments then called into the house, "C'mon Stephen. C'mon, Mother. Christina and Jenny are already at the pool."

Over the past couple of days, the initial shock and fear of their situation had worn off for Allie and the kids. Although not exactly a blessing in disguise, the unexpected holiday in Florida was beginning to feel like a vacation.

Stephen and Allie's mother, Helen, came outside together. Stephen had a bemused look on his face; his grandmother was telling him, nonstop, about the many varieties and benefits of Polish cooking. Stephen, already thinking about a medical career, tried to suggest that such cooking might be a bit hearty to eat very often.

"Nonsense," exclaimed Helen. "Researchers are beginning to find that cabbage is one of the healthiest foods in the world. And what do you think makes Polish women so pretty?"

"But not necessarily cooked that way, Grandma," Stephen said kindly.

At this point in their conversation, they joined Allie and began to walk the few blocks to the neighborhood pool.

Allie's mother lived in a pleasant section of Clearwater, made up largely of small but very attractive homes occupied by retired people. Her parents had moved south almost immediately after her father's retirement. He had died about ten years earlier, a few years after he had retired. Helen had a terrible time at first, but after a few years, she began to make the adjustment to living alone. Now she was doing very well.

As they walked, Allie was thinking about how good it was to see the kids spend some time with their grandmother. And the kids seemed to be genuinely enjoying it too. Helen especially liked Stephen's company, probably because he was a very good listener.

"Now, Stephen," she was continuing, "when you're a big shot doctor, don't be too quick to listen to all these so-called new ideas..."

"Yes, Grandma," Stephen offered.

They arrived at the pool and walked through the gate. By now, the attendants knew they were Helen's guests and so made no inquiries about them. Christina and Jenny were standing in the water. Christina seemed to be offering advice to Jenny, probably about her boyfriend. Allie thought with relief, *Maybe Christina can give her good advice; she certainly won't listen to me.*

Stephen spotted the clothes and towels which his sisters had brought with them.

"Over there, Mom. It looks like they saved some chairs for us."

Allie, Helen, and Stephen walked to the chairs and settled into them. There weren't many people at the pool today. There seldom were. The retired people in the neighborhood did not seem to be active swimmers. Two uniformed workmen, wearing sunglasses, were testing and cleaning the water. Perhaps 10 to 15 people were sitting around the pool in groups of two or three. Another handful, including the two girls, were in the water.

When the girls saw the rest of their family get settled in the chairs, they came out of the water and joined them.

"I'd get to know him a lot better first, Jenny," Christina was saying.

They had attracted Allie's attention. "What's that?

First before what?"

The two girls looked at their mother and then at each other and began laughing.

"We're talking about Jim and Jenny going together, Mom."

"Oh," Allie said.

The girls were getting into good suntanning positions. Allie and Stephen were reading. And Helen was deciding which of her two granddaughters most needed her advice and counsel.

They were all together, and this is what the two workmen had been waiting for. With a quick exchange of glances and a brief nod, they dropped what they were doing, and began to slowly move toward the family.

Simultaneously, the couple who had told the attendants they were guests of the Carsons, and had produced their membership card to prove it, moved in the same direction.

Then everything happened very quickly.

The workmen drew their weapons and pointed at the family. They were within 15 feet of the Sandlers.

Stephen was the first to see them.

"Mom! Watch out!" Stephen yelled as he began to move off the chair.

Allie, the girls, and Helen first looked at Stephen and then in the direction of his movement.

At that instant, they heard shots, and both workmen were hit. They fell in a heap on the tiled pool surface.

Screams echoed from around the pool, including those from Allie and the girls. As they surveyed the fallen men, practically at their feet, blood appeared beneath and around them. Helen just looked, eyes wide, unable to speak.

They barely noticed the man and woman, standing near them, still searching the crowd and surroundings for any further danger.

Still watching for any additional threat, the man said, "I'm sorry we couldn't tell you we were here to help out, Mrs. Sandler. We thought it best that way. Sidney Harrison asked us to keep an eye on you."

"Mother, look." Jenny was pointing to one of the slain men. They could not see the man's face, but Jenny pointed out a large, turquoise ring on the dead man's outstretched hand.

White as a sheet and with a slight tremble, Allie asked in an agonized voice, "Would they... did they mean to kill us all?"

"We'll never know the answer to that, Mrs. Sandler," the man replied now meeting her gaze for the first time.

Then Allie volunteered, "I don't want my husband to

know about this. It won't help him. It will only slow him down. We'll all go somewhere else. But I don't want him to know."

"Mrs. Sandler," said the woman bodyguard, "we can arrange for your safety. There is a place we would like to take you and your family where it will be safe."

"Let's go then," replied Allie rather meekly, but then perking up, "But first, I hope you don't mind if I check out your story with Mr. Harrison?"

Handing Allie his cellular phone, she replied, "I think that would be quite prudent under the circumstances."

Allie confirmed the couple's story with Sidney Harrison. After thanking him for the added protection, Allie hung up. She then turned to the two bodyguards and agreed to go wherever they felt would be safe.

28

Paul had come to Phoenix for two reasons: to talk with the mysterious Dr. Alfred Holstein and to check out those damned roses. Paul had the name of Dr. Alfred Holstein, but that was all he had. No address. No phone number. Still, he considered, how hard could it be to locate a practicing physician?

Quite hard, as it turned out. Mostly because Dr. Holstein was no longer in practice. As near as Paul could tell, Holstein didn't have a very big practice to begin with. Apparently, he had plenty of money and accepted only those patients with a strong personal or professional attachment. Now, however, Paul found the physician's office completely closed with a sign on the office door simply stating, "Dr. Alfred Holstein Has Closed His Practice."

Paul then returned to the phone book to check for a residential listing. There was none. Nor could the phone company help.

Finally, in desperation he went door-to-door in the office building where Dr. Holstein had his office. No one seemed to know anything about the physician until, now really at his wit's end, Paul visited the electronics store on the ground floor.

"I'm trying to locate Dr. Alfred Holstein," he said to the store manager. "He used to have an office on the third floor, but has closed it. Do you know him?"

"Sure do," she responded. "He's a good customer. A real music nut."

"Can you help me find him?"

"Well," the manager began, "we've sold him lots of equipment over the years. I suppose we have his home address. But I just can't give out that kind of information."

Paul was ready for this, and getting better and better at playing detective.

"Please. My daughter is in Dr. Holstein's care and is very ill. I can't get her prescription refilled without his OK. I must find him."

"Well, I guess that's different."

And so, she gave Paul the doctor's home address.

Finding Holstein's address took a great deal more time than Paul had bargained for, but it had to be done. He parked his rental car in front of 517 Campfire Drive, turned off the engine, and looked around. A gorgeous location. He was looking down on Phoenix from a hilltop south of the city. It was dusk now, and the city's lights were beginning to come on. The neighborhood was beautiful, with western-type stucco houses in various shades of pink, rust, and gold, with mauve colored tile roofs. Here and there, beautifully blended, were small professional and office buildings.

Paul got out of the car, went up the walk to the front door, and rang the bell, but there was no answer.

"Damn," Paul exclaimed. Would he never find this guy? He rang again. Still no answer. He listened closely and thought he heard talking from within.

Paul had never walked into a house under such circumstances. But, driven now by his sense of urgency and frustration, he tried the door. It was unlocked.

"Hello," he called as he entered the foyer. "Hello?"

Although no one responded, Paul definitely heard talking in the house.

He moved cautiously as he walked further down the entrance hallway.

"Anyone home? Dr. Holstein?"

The man standing in the shadows had intended to

leave the house unseen, but now his path was blocked and he would be discovered, ruining everything. Panicked, he lunged at Paul intending to bring his gun down hard on Paul's head.

Sensing, more than seeing, the arm coming at him in the dim hallway, Paul simultaneously dipped, turned, and raised his arm, deflecting the blow. The intruder was a big man. Surprised at Paul's move, he grabbed Paul and hurled him further down the hallway. Paul ricocheted off the wall, falling in a heap at the entrance to the kitchen.

At first, the man seemed unsure what to do next. Then, slowly, he raised his gun and aimed it at Paul. Instinctively, looking for a weapon, a shield, or anything to protect himself, Paul grabbed the throw-rug lining the hallway and pulled hard. The man flew into the air as he lost his footing, gun shots spraying the walls and ceiling. He landed hard, letting out a cry of pain, and dropped the gun.

Paul began to rise and move toward the gun, but the man limped rapidly out the door and hurried away.

Slowly regaining his composure, Paul moved in the direction of the voices. As he moved toward the sound, Paul realized the voices were coming from a television.

He entered the living room. Dr. Holstein was sitting on the sofa facing the TV screen. He seemed to be asleep, although Paul couldn't imagine anyone sleeping through the fight and gunshots only a few yards away.

"Dr. Holstein?"

Paul raise his voice a bit.

"Dr. Holstein."

He approached the unmoving figure, reached out, touched his shoulder and shook him gently.

Backing away as the man fell to his side on the sofa, Paul gasped, "Oh my God."

There were no marks Paul could see. No blood. No weapons. No signs of a scuffle.

After his nerves settled down and Paul absorbed what had happened, he began to look around. Almost at once, he noticed a handwritten note on the coffee table in front of the sofa. Paul picked it up. The note read:

To Whom It May Concern:

I was President Alexander Rose's personal physician in 1978 when the assassination attempt on his life occurred. As the world knows, the President received severe head wounds. The world also believes he died of those wounds. He did not. I perceived that the President was likely to live, basically in a vegetative state, for many years. Alexander Rose was my friend, as well as my President, and I could not allow that to happen. So I ended his life.

In this I acted alone, without the knowledge or con-

sent of any other party. I can no longer go on with this enormous guilt and so have taken the same way out I used for my friend.

The note was signed, *Alfred Holstein, M.D.*

"So that's it," Paul said softly.

Then Paul sat on a chair and thought again, reviewing in his mind all that had transpired. *Dr. Holstein was afraid of being discovered due to some fluke payments uncovered by an audit. Payments for roses for... A grave? A memorial for the President? To stop the audit, Stefie and me, he went to all kinds of lengths to frighten and intimidate... He's a murderer, or hired others to do his killing. We wouldn't stop, so he... gave it up.*

Or, and the hair tingled on Paul's neck as he thought... *or, others helped the doctor. Knew what he did. Maybe even... even persuaded him to end the President's life. So others are involved. Others? But who? And if others are involved...*

For the first time since he began this assignment, Paul knew what to do next. He began by phoning the police to tell them to come to 517 Campfire Drive in The Peake.

Next, he phoned the airport to arrange a flight to Washington. And then he phoned his secretary at home in Cleveland and asked her to set up a meeting for him in Washington.

29

Paul's posture with the Phoenix police had been to tell the truth, if not the whole truth. Essentially, he had shown them identification and told them where and how he could be reached.

"I am a CPA, performing an audit for my firm, and was planning to interview Dr. Holstein. When I arrived here this evening, I found him like this."

There had been some discussion of the note written by Dr. Holstein, and as to Dr. Holstein's mental state when he wrote it. Paul figured he needed another day, perhaps two, and he would have that much time before any serious attention would be given to the note, the Federal authorities were brought in, or the media involved.

Paul returned to his hotel room for a short nap. He

was scheduled to take the "red eye" to Washington in a few hours and hoped to get some rest before then. He set the alarm so he could make his 11 p.m. flight. Before he could doze off, the phone rang.

"Mr. Sandler, this is Roberta Glover. I'm a friend of John Barlow and I'm investigating Peter Wilson's death. I heard that Dr. Holstein turned up dead."

"Yes, Ms. Glover, I heard that too," replied Paul.

There was a long pause and Roberta continued. "John Barlow suggested that we should get together and compare notes. You know, maybe we can fill the gaps in each other's stories."

Paul shifted uneasily as he struggled with how much, if any, information he should reveal to Ms. Glover. She was right though—it would be nice to know what she knew. Maybe he could get some more answers. Paul agreed saying, "I will just promise to listen. Let's meet in my hotel lobby in a half hour."

Paul finished packing, arranged for a late check-out, and sat down in a corner chair in the lobby. He had no idea what she looked like, but since only a few people were there, he hoped spotting Ms. Glover would be easy. In a few minutes, a tall dark-haired woman walked into the lobby and looked around.

"Ms. Glover?" Paul ventured.

"Yes. Please, it's Roberta. Paul Sandler, I assume?"

Paul rose and shook her hand. "It looks more private in the cafe. Would you like to talk there?" Paul asked.

Roberta nodded and followed Paul into the cafe. Once seated, Roberta immediately pulled out her notebook. "Well I don't have much, Mr. Sandler."

"Please, call me Paul."

"All right. I've been busy dealing with Peter Wilson's remains, but I did have a chance to go through his notebook. It was left in his rental car the night he died. The most interesting part is that several pages have been ripped out. But, Pete's pen left a few indentations in the notebook's cardboard backing. These indented words do not appear in any of the remaining pages, so I assumed then that they were from the last page that was ripped out."

"Wait," said Paul, "how do you know Mr. Wilson didn't rip them out himself? Maybe whatever was written on them was not useful, so he threw the pages away."

"Most reporters don't rip pages out of their notebooks because you never know what might become important. Some seemingly trivial fact you recorded early in the investigation could turn out to be the key to the story. Since Pete was a very careful and thorough reporter, I don't think he ripped these pages out himself. Plus, when I picked-up his belongings, it was obvious that they had been sifted through more than once."

Paul thought, *She is probably right. We had several*

pages of the audit removed from our file. "Tell me more about those imprinted words."

"One word looks like it says 'Evergreen' and the other just says 'government funds'."

Paul Sandler shook his head. "Evergreen means nothing to me and government funds is so broad—who knows?"

Earlier in the day, Glover conducted a Lexis-Nexis search to check not-for-profit incorporations and found an Evergreen Foundation that was established to make grants to nursing homes. Glover thought, *Okay, he doesn't know about the Evergreen Foundation, and he also doesn't know that the Chairperson of the Evergreen Foundation is Marian Rose. I think I'll save that for myself.*

"Oh," Roberta said, " the name Harold Johnson has surfaced. This name also comes up on some of the prescription orders that were copied for us and sent to John Barlow via his informant."

Again, Paul shook his head. "I don't know a Harold Johnson, but I'll write down his name in case I come across it."

"That's all I have for you. Do you have anything to tell me?" Roberta asked bluntly.

Paul hesitated, "Until the audit's finished, I can't... "

"Hold on," interrupted Roberta, "I know all that crap,

just tell me what you can."

Paul decided that what he had said to the police about Holstein's death was not part of the audit, so he repeated that information to her.

"BS!" mumbled Roberta

"Excuse me?" said Paul.

"No way could the Doctor work alone. Furthermore, a Harold Johnson is connected in some way with this whole mess."

Paul, now completely exhausted only shook his head again.

"Well," said Roberta, "here is my number in Phoenix. Call if you think we can be of use to each other."

Paul headed up to his room for a much needed nap and to prepare for his flight to Washington. Unfortunately, the nap was too short.

30

When Paul arrived in Washington, it was the beginning of the business day there. He checked into his hotel and called to update Sidney Harrison on his progress.

The next morning, he rose early and refreshed. When he arrived at the White House, he spent a few minutes in his office and then set out for Frank Norman's office. He arrived promptly at 11 a.m., as he had hoped.

"Hello, Mr. Sandler. You've been a very busy man. And widely traveled from all I hear," Frank Norman commented as he motioned Paul to a chair. "You showed good judgment in asking for this meeting."

"And just how much do you hear, Mr. Norman," Paul asked as he sat down.

"Everything. That's how I serve the President."

"And his sister?"

"Paul. May I call you, Paul? You need to know a few things about how this place works."

"I'm learning fast, Frank."

"I am afraid not fast enough. I am Special Assistant to the President, and have been for his two terms of office. Before that, I was his Special Assistant when he was Vice President. Even then my boss had unusual access to President Huggard, and I did too. Under my arrangement with President Rose, I am his Chief of Staff as well as his Special Assistant. I tell you all this, Paul, not to explain my clout or authority—I've been around the White House too long for that—but to explain the way it is. It is important that you understand some things. Get to know us better. Perhaps even be on our side."

"An auditor doesn't take sides, Frank. He may end up being an umpire, although he doesn't mean to be. He reminds the players of the rules. He helps keep the game straight."

"Auditor. Auditor. C'mon, Paul. You make a very good living. But don't you want more? Have you no dreams?"

"No, I don't. I guess I have a flaw in my character. I like what I do. It's honest work. I help keep the system moving and on track. And I have all the money I need."

"Let me continue, Paul. For all my, my..."

"Power?" Paul offered.

"For all my influence, it pales in significance when compared to that held by the President's sister. I mean no disrespect to President Rose. He would agree when I tell you that they are really co-Presidents. There have been jokes in the media to this effect, and of course, we ignore or deny them. But the truth goes well beyond these stories."

"I thought in America," Paul ventured, "you were supposed to run for office if you wanted the kind of power you're talking about."

"Power, power. You keep saying power, Paul. Forget power. We're talking influence. C'mon, Paul, get with it. Didn't you ever watch a congressional committee hearing and observe your precious elected officials in action? Without their key staff people, those guys couldn't function. Most of them don't know the answers or the questions. Many don't even know the issues, or why they're there at all. These klutzes have the power, but we—the staff people, the friends—have the influence."

"And, therefore, the real power," Paul added.

"If you wish," affirmed Frank Norman.

"That's not the system; it's a breakdown in the system. It needs fixing."

"But, that's the way it is today, Paul, for you and for

me. And we, the influencers and friends, need your help. The stakes are very high."

Even though, presumably, this was his meeting, Paul felt he ought to follow this dialogue wherever it would lead.

"Just what is it you want of me, Mr. Norman?"

"Frank. I want you to hear our story and I want you to help us."

"Us?"

Frank Norman pressed a bell under his desk. He sat in silence. Within a minute, perhaps two, Marian Rose walked in.

31

Marian Rose or, as the opposition press had dubbed her, "The Dragon Lady," walked into the room. She sat in the chair next to Paul, in front of Frank Norman's desk.

She was a woman approaching 70 years of age, a few years older than her brother, Jonathan, who was now close to completion of his second term as President. She was slender, tall, and seemed very fit for a woman of her age, but gave off a cold, icy presence.

Marian Rose nodded in Paul's direction and began, "Have you gotten to know us, Paul? We desperately need your help."

"Know you. Ms. Rose? I'm not sure what you mean," Paul was bewildered.

"Please call me Marian. We think when you know us, understand why we've done certain things, you will want to help us."

Marian Rose continued, "I am certain Frank has told you about his devotion to my brother as both Vice President and President. Actually it goes far beyond that. He was very close to my brother Alexander before he... before he died. He also served Vice President Huggard faithfully when Alexander was President. Not an easy role, to be the confidant of both the President and his Vice President."

Rising from her chair and walking to the window, she continued, "Frank admired these men and their policies. Therefore he wished to serve them. But my role has been a different one. And my motivations quite different too. Bub and Jonny...," she corrected herself, "... family nicknames. Alexander and Jonathan were, are, my brothers. I have served them, and this country, out of my love for them. Believe it or not, Paul, I have had numerous opportunities for romance and marriage over the years. But long ago, I made a decision to assist my brothers in what we all knew would be brilliant political careers. I decided to forego my own personal interests, personal life."

"Ms. Rose. Marian. I appreciate your frankness, but I don't see what this has to do with my audit."

"You will, Paul."

She continued as she turned her gaze on Paul, "To understand, really understand, what happened, and why we did what we did, you need to recall the way the world and the U.S. were then. The Cold War. Deficits. Unrest. Vietnam. Inflation. That's why we did it."

"Did... Did what?"

"Killed my brother. Bub... President Alexander Rose."

Paul whispered, hoarsely, "You what?"

Paul looked at Frank Norman. He was nodding, smiling, agreeing. Frank Norman is on the brink, Paul was thinking, but this woman is 100 percent insane.

Marian Rose continued, "*Kill* is a strong word. We simply let the President die. More precisely, we helped him die."

"But..." Paul started, "But...why? I don't understand."

Marian continued, "Alexander was injured beyond hope for recovery in the assassination attempt, but could have sustained life in an incapacitated state for many years with constant medical care. We, I, couldn't let that happen. Not for the sake of the country. How would the Presidency function? What would happen during the inevitable period of confusion? I couldn't, wouldn't let that happen to my big brother."

"And Alfred Holstein helped you."

"He was our instrument. He knew which drugs to use."

"Did you also... did you kill Dr. Holstein?"

"That's not important, Paul, and has nothing to do with you helping us."

"Why do you tell me all this now?"

"Because," she continued, "when you know the full story, you will understand and help."

Frank Norman was still nodding in agreement and smiling.

"My God. There's more?"

"We worked it out to see the country through the bad times. Vice President Huggard would be sworn in immediately as President. He would name Jonathan as his Vice President. After all, he was in Alexander's cabinet. We figured in the confusion and grief of the assassination, Dave would be a shoo-in for the next presidential election, and then Jonathan would eventually be elected in his own right. And that's exactly the way it worked out."

And with that, Marian Rose and Frank Norman smiled at each other.

Paul waited, unsure of what to say or do. Then he decided to break the silence, "And... and what is it you expect of me?"

Frank Norman finally spoke, "You could simply count your little financial audit as done and issue your firm's opinion. You could then continue with the performance audit. We would write a most generous contract. And there could be much more for you personally." Norman concluded, "You can see it now, can't you Paul? We helped President Rose and we helped the country."

"And you didn't do too badly for yourselves, either," added Paul.

Frank Norman looked genuinely puzzled, "What do you mean?"

Ignoring the warning signals that were flashing inside him, Paul let some of his anger out. "Forgive me if I'm missing something here, but all these actions on behalf of big brother and the country allowed for the two of you to stay in positions of power—make that influence—for a very long, long time. Actions, by the way, which included murder, mayhem, blackmail, and God knows what else. Not that it matters, but how much does little brother Jonny know about all this?"

"You know more than he does," responded Frank Norman, almost cryptically.

"And Dave Huggard?"

"Of course, he needed to know the whole thing," responded Norman. "Given all we knew about him and his background, it was in his best interests to go along. Paul?"

"Yeah, Frank?"

"Does this mean you won't help us?"

Paul felt fear welling up in his throat.

"I misunderstood Mr. Sandler, Frank," interjected Marian Rose. "I thought he was smart, a good American. I thought he cared about this administration, our country. I was wrong. He does not want to help us. Am I correct, Mr. Sandler?"

"I came here, and Stephanie Hamilton came here, to complete an audit of White House funds. I don't understand all the intricacies of politics, of games of power, or influence, or whatever you want to call it. But I know when a trust has been violated. When public monies have been used improperly, that's my business and I'm good at it.

Paul wanted to say more, but held back. It was too late to give this pair a lecture on American values. Then Paul stood up, preparing to leave.

"You know, of course, we can't let you complete this audit," interjected Frank Norman.

"I'll discuss our options with my senior partner and let you know," said Paul, more determined than ever to get to the bottom of this for the sake of his family, Stefie, and his country.

And with that, Paul turned and walked out of the office.

32

Paul knew, or at least believed, he was safe as long as he was in the White House. For one thing, there were a great many people—make that witnesses—around. But he would not want to bet on his chances of survival once outside. He pondered his next move as he walked back to his office. It was still only early afternoon, so Paul figured he had some time to think things through.

He had not seen Sarah Harding, Frank Norman's secretary, much at all, but she now met him and informed him that several auditors, representatives of Dodney, Harrison had displayed their credentials and were waiting for him in his office. She had not been informed in advance, and she let Paul know this was most irregular. Paul tried to be nonchalant, "Thank you, Ms. Harding. I should have given you some warning."

When he reached his office, two men Paul had never seen before—definitely not auditors, but maybe former pro-football players—were waiting for him outside the door. Somehow they recognized him, said "Hello," and opened his office door. He was reluctant to enter.

When he did so, slowly, two more large men were waiting inside. They didn't merely occupy a chair or two; they filled the room.

One of the men, accepted as the leader, greeted Paul. "Hello, Mr. Sandler. We're here to give you any help you may need. Sidney Harrison sent us. He also sent a message which I don't fully understand. I'm to remind you that someone wanting a job with Dodney, Harrison, and a partnership, ought not to order lobster unless he knows how to eat it."

At first Paul was confused. Then he remembered, and smiled. When he was interviewed by the firm for a position, a good many years back, and then for a partnership, years later, he persistently ordered lobster for dinner both times. Not many people order a whole lobster in Cleveland and, if they do, they know how to eat it. Paul did not know how, and proved it both times. But only a few people knew about this inside joke. These men were sent by Sidney Harrison, Paul concluded with relief.

Now sensing the message had worked, the man added, "I'm Jerome Branson. We are to stay here to help you. Or, if you wish, we have a charter plane available at Washington National to take you to Cleveland, or wherever you need to go. One more thing, Mr. Sandler. Mr. Harrison wants me to tell you that your family is fine. They had some trouble, and are no longer in Clearwater, but they are safe. He's keeping a close watch over them. Here's Mr. Harrison's home phone number and a cellular phone. It's equipped with a scrambler, so any calls you make will be secure. Mr. Harrison says to call him if you want to discuss it further."

Whether it was the reinforcements and the security they provided, or being reminded of his family's plight, Paul determined then and there to end this nightmare quickly. He asked their help in packing up the working papers and getting them to a waiting car. Then they all left— for good Paul earnestly hoped—and headed for the airport.

Paul had one more trip to make—back to Arizona. If his instincts were correct, this trip would end the audit and perhaps a great many other things as well.

Once they reached the airport, Branson led Sandler to a private conference room in the Admiral's Club. Branson and Sandler sat down while the others waited outside. "Mr. Sandler, we're not just bodyguards, but a team of security professionals. I am an attorney, spent time as a Secret Service Agent, and now head one of Washington's most respected personal security services as part of my law practice. I know that sounds pompous, but that's the way it is. Here is a letter of agreement describing our confidential attorney-client relationship with Dodney, Harrison. By contract, we are agents of your firm and, among other things, have agreed to be bound by your code of ethics on this assignment. In order for us to provide you with the best protection and the best legal representation, we need to know everything about this audit engagement. Sidney Harrison has already briefed me on everything he knows and asks in this note that you do the same."

Paul read the note and asked, "Why did you leave the Secret Service?"

Branson looked down, "I was part of the team that guarded President Alexander Rose. I admired and trusted him very much. You could see his integrity every time you looked into his eyes. I wasn't on duty the day he was killed, but his death disturbed me greatly."

Paul then went into great detail and explained everything.

Across from the White House, Roberta Glover waited patiently for Sandler to appear. When she saw Paul Sandler being rushed to a waiting limousine by the head of Washington's premier executive protection service, she hailed a cab and followed Sandler to the airport. At the airport, she called Barlow immediately. "Something big is happening. Sandler just left the White House with Jerome Branson. I followed them to the airport. They're going somewhere on a chartered plane," she explained excitedly.

John Barlow knew that Jerome Branson was a legend, both as a specialist in the most sensitive executive protection matters and as an attorney representing clients with delicate Federal government concerns. Branson had connections through all branches of the Federal government. "Use your investigative skills to get the flight plan and follow them wherever they go," bellowed Barlow.

After several time-consuming delays, Roberta Glover caught a plane to Phoenix, Arizona. Upon arrival, she happened to rent the same maroon Dodge Intrepid that she had on her previous trip.

33

By a colossal combination of bad luck, coincidences, and White House plotting, no one had yet gotten to the bottom of the use of several improper checks to pay for the delivery of roses. That, after all, was what initially triggered all that had transpired. Stephanie Hamilton was murdered as she began to ask questions about the payments, threatening a trip to Phoenix. A reporter had died trying to answer these same questions. And Paul himself, on his first trip to Phoenix, had virtually flipped a coin and decided to hunt down Alfred Holstein first. When he had found the doctor dead, he immediately left Phoenix. This time, Paul resolved, nothing would deter him from tracking down the flower payments and completing his work. And, auditors or not, the beefy group he had brought with him to Phoenix gave him considerable reassurance.

During the flight, Paul planned his next steps in considerable detail. He also tried to clarify his responsibilities by turning to the *Yellow Book*. Some passages leaped out at him. One related to "indirect illegal acts," or acts having material but indirect effects on the financial statements. Paul read:

Auditors should be aware of the possibility that indirect illegal acts may have occurred. If specific information comes to the auditors' attention that provides evidence concerning the existence of possible illegal acts that could have a material indirect effect on the financial statements, the auditors should apply audit procedures specifically directed to ascertaining whether an illegal act has occurred.

Another *Yellow Book* passage read:

Auditors should exercise due professional care in pursuing indications of possible irregularities and illegal acts so as not to interfere with potential future investigations, legal proceedings, or both. Under some circumstances, laws, regulations, or policies may require auditors to report indications of certain types of irregularities or illegal acts to law enforcement or investigatory authorities before extending audit steps and procedures. Auditors may also be required to withdraw from or defer further work on the audit or a portion of the audit in order not to interfere with an investigation.

Paul realized that he had several options open to him at this point, including withdrawing from or postponing the audit. However, he chose to continue, for Stefie's sake, as well as his own reluctance to bend to pressure. *Here's hoping*, he thought, *ol' Sidney's checking with the firm's lawyers.*

When they arrived in Phoenix, they could not do anything until the following day since it was already after dinnertime. So they took hotel rooms for the night. Early the next morning they were on their way. Their first stop was May's Flowers, the florist shop shown on a few of the invoices they could locate in the records. Paul and his new "friend" Jerome walked into the store. The others waited outside in the van Jerome had rented. A van was apparently the only vehicle that could comfortably accommodate Paul, Jerome and the other members of the security team.

"Hi, I'm Paul Sandler, and I need some help. Over the past several months there've been a large number of flowers purchased here. We don't know where they are being delivered, but there's been a mix up in funds. You may have been receiving payment from an incorrect source, and we are just trying to get it straightened out. No one will take any money away from you, as long as it is legally due to you. And I'm sure it is."

"Good God, are you guys still horsing around with that? I'm Bill Petrie. I own this shop."

"What do you mean," asked Paul.

"A guy was in here a week or two ago asking the

same questions. He talked to one of my part-time workers and disappeared before I could talk to him."

"You know how the government is," commented Paul, shaking his head.

"OK. We really liked the business, and we gave them a good price. A rose every doggone day of the year. I've suggested other flowers, say mums or daisies, but nothing doing. What do you need to know?"

Finally, Paul thought. "Who orders them?"

"I don't know. It was a standing order. Goes back a long way. We are well-located, and we have a good reputation in the city. I've only owned the store eight or nine years. The order came with the business. We were paid regularly. Used to be a foundation paid us. Then it switched for a time to the U.S. Government. I'm just selling flowers. I don't want to mess with the government."

Finally, Paul asked the most important question. "Mr. Petrie," he began, "it is very important that we know what is happening to all these flowers. Where are they going?"

"Now, that's an easy one. Damned expensive to run a fresh rose to the same place each day of the year, year in and year out. We'd hardly forget. They all go to the same place, out at The Peake."

Paul felt his skin tingle, remembering his trip to Dr. Holstein's home.

"That's a resort community south of town. There is a very small and expensive nursing home in The Peake. Hold on. It's at 701 Wagon Wheel Road. We don't know who the flowers are for, but they seem to know there. Our informal contacts right now tell us the roses are going to a Mr. Harold Johnson, but that changes from time to time. Look, is there going to be any trouble?"

"Thanks for your help, Mr. Petrie. No, you are not in any trouble. We just need to get this squared away."

And they left May's Flowers and headed east and then south to The Peake. Paul hoped this visit would be more helpful than the first trip there, when he found Dr. Holstein dead.

34

When they arrived at the proper address, they parked in a small parking area at the side of the building. Except for the parking area and a bit more activity than usual, it looked like the other homes and professional buildings in the area. There was no sign to indicate this was a nursing facility.

Paul and Jerome walked to the building while one of his “friends” stayed with the car, and the other scouted the perimeter of the building.

Paul rang the bell at the front door. The door was opened by a well-dressed, if burly, attendant in a white jacket and pants.

“Yes?”

“I’d like to speak to someone in charge, please.”

Offended, the attendant responded, “I’m in charge. What is it you want?”

Paul decided to move ahead. “I want to see Mr. Harold Johnson.”

The attendant seemed puzzled, and then smiled. He looked Paul and Jerome over, and made a decision.

“Come in. I’ll ask my supervisor to see you.”

The attendant disappeared. Paul and his companion stood in the foyer for a few minutes. From the outside, this looked like many other large homes, Paul reflected. But that was not the case on the inside. This building was a genuine, if small and plush, nursing home. At least, it had the appearance of such a facility, including a few attendants and nurses moving about several offices and other rooms down a hallway, a couple of large rooms with windows overlooking the city, which seemed designed as visiting rooms, and the faint odor of medicine and antiseptic. The only thing missing was... “Patients,” Paul whispered to Jerome. “Where are the patients?” Jerome followed Paul’s gaze down the empty corridors but remained silent.

Just then a woman in a nurse’s uniform approached them.

“Hello, I’m Janice White. I’m the supervisor in charge during the day. Arnold says there is some confusion.”

"Ms. White, I'm Paul Sandler. I'm not at all confused, but we have a very strange story here which we need to get cleared up. I won't try to fool you. We are not from the police. We are all from a well-known Cleveland, Ohio, CPA firm named Dodney, Harrison. This may sound strange to you, but as part of our work we are trying to track down the expenditure of several thousand dollars for roses. From what we can tell, a fresh rose is delivered to this address each day. For a Mr. Johnson. We need to confirm this information to complete our audit."

The attendant had apparently been waiting nearby, listening to Paul's speech. Sensing the insistence in Paul's voice, he reentered the room and stood beside Janice White.

"It's all right, Arnold. I'll take care of it." The attendant left.

"Mr. Sandler. Let me try to help clarify things. We have nothing to hide. First of all, we are not like any kind of nursing home you have probably ever seen, nor are you likely to ever see one quite like this one again. If we had not had the support of very strong friends, we could never have opened this building in The Peake. When we began nearly twenty years ago, we planned to handle as many as eight or ten patients, all of course, from very wealthy, exclusive families. However, in fact, we have never had more than one patient. We don't know why, and we have never asked. I suppose it is simply too great an expense even for very affluent families.

It costs several million dollars each year to keep the doors opened. Someone pays the bills. Of course, we on the staff have a wonderful arrangement. Lastly, we have had the privilege of having as our head physician, a gentleman who has been the personal physician to more than one U.S. President."

She hasn't heard yet, Paul thought. *I wonder how they kept that quiet.*

White beamed with pride. "We are, all in all, a very fine institution, if an unusual one."

"Then your sole patient is Harold Johnson?"

"I'm afraid that's a bad joke on our part, Mr. Sandler. There is no record of his real name, even though his expenses are always paid promptly," and she became a bit more serious. "A bad joke that got away from us. Because we have expected additional patients over the years, but have never received them, we began to give our only patient various names. It confuses the flower delivery man. As I say, a bad joke."

So, Paul thought, *what do I do now?*

"Can we see Mr. Johnson?" Paul asked.

"I don't see any problem with that. The poor man has no family, no friends. Someone pays the bills, but no one ever bothers to visit him. Except, of course, for his physician, Dr. Holstein."

As Nurse White walked down the hall, she described

the small laboratory, the pool and other features of the facility. "We even have a director of security, but who knows why? The foundation that funds us insists it is necessary. He has been out of town lately, but no one minds. We have no security problems and he seems kind of spooky."

Paul froze when he read the sign on the next door — Robert Parish, Director of Security.

"Here is our only patient," White said as she continued down the hall to the next room.

She ushered Paul and his colleague into a sitting room, just the kind of room one would expect to find in this building. It was very nice with a wonderful view of the city, connecting to a bedroom. The furnishings were unusually rich for a care facility.

As they walked into the bedroom, White noted, "He doesn't communicate because of the heavy sedation."

Paul looked at the man in the bed. His whole presence, demeanor, were shocking. He was fastened to his bed, seemingly to keep him from falling. He seemed to be an elderly man, 70 or even older, although it was nearly impossible to be sure. He had a full head of hair and, at one time, might have been a handsome man, except for the massive scarring that distorted his features, pulling the skin unnaturally tight on the left side of his face. His gaze was intense—his eyes blinked, but he never moved or changed a facial expression. All in all, it was, Paul decided, sad and horrifying.

"Why is his face scarred that way?" Paul asked.

"I understand he had tragic and serious facial injuries," replied Ms. White.

"And there is no record of who he is?"

"No. We only know he is a man from a very wealthy family which wants to help him, and can afford to do so, but won't or can't come to see him. All contacts are through a trust of some sort. Perhaps all family members are now dead."

"Does he... Does he never move?" Paul asked Ms. White.

"Only a few times during the 15 years I've worked here. Dr. Holstein's orders are to always keep him heavily sedated. He becomes violent and delusional otherwise," Ms. White stated as she went to the corner of the room and began pushing a wheelchair toward the bed.

"Delusional?" Paul asked.

"Yes, it's quite sad, really." She began to untie the restraints.

Paul was uncertain. What did this man have to do with Washington? How was he involved in Marian's plot? Who was sending the roses and why? Screw the roses, Paul decided. The President's sister and Special Assistant had admitted to murder. The murder of

President Alexander Rose. And the other killings shouldn't be too tough to prove either. Prove? Proof? How much was there? What a nightmare. What would it take to expose these people?

Paul found himself walking around the room, then stopping to flip through the pages of a book on a table in the room. A Bible. *Good*, Paul thought. *Just what I need.* He flipped through a few more pages and then noticed handwriting inside the front cover. He read:

June 30, 1937

To Bub,

Happy Birthday, big brother, and here is your gift. You were so sweet to send me a rose a day when I was ill.

I love you. One day I'll return the kindness.

Love,

Marian

Paul closed the Bible and looked toward the man in the bed. *Alexander Rose*, he almost blurted out in shock. He knew he had discovered the secret that Marian Rose and Frank Norman had tried so viciously to protect. Paul's mind started to reel as he considered the heinousness of the crime and the enormity of the coverup. He struggled to contain his outrage as he felt his fear beginning to escalate. *I've got to keep my wits and focus on getting us out of here quickly and safely.* He promptly calmed himself and thought more about his situation.

He had uncovered clear evidence of an illegal act. He knew that under the *Yellow Book* guidelines, his responsibility as an auditor was complete. Taking any further action might interfere with future legal proceedings. But Paul believed Frank Norman's threat to stop the audit at whatever cost, and he would not let this past President share Dr. Holstein's fate.

Nurse White was tending to her patient when she interrupted Paul's train of thought, "I need to get an attendant to help lift Mr. Johnson into the wheelchair. I'm getting ready to take the patient out onto the rear grounds for a walk. If you want to talk further, you'll have to join us."

"Why thank you, we'd be pleased to," replied Paul as he motioned to Jerome and tried to collect his thoughts.

"I'll help lift Mr. Johnson," Jerome volunteered.

As Nurse White was fastening her patient to the wheelchair, Paul gave the Bible to Jerome and pointed out the inscription. Jerome flinched when he read the Bible and looked over at Alexander Rose. Paul then whispered, "Bring the van to the back of the building for a pick-up."

A determined Jerome met Paul's gaze, nodded, pocketed the Bible and left the room.

35

As Ms. White pushed the wheelchair to the edge of the property, the van appeared and Jerome stepped out. "Sorry, Ms. White, I know that this is inconvenient, but Mr. Johnson is being transferred immediately." The two other burly men jumped out of the van and picked up the wheelchair and put it, along with its passenger, into the van.

Outnumbered and surrounded, Nurse White turned and ran back to the facility, calling for help. The van raced down the driveway, swerving to avoid the rear seats that had been tossed out moments earlier.

An approaching maroon Dodge Intrepid narrowly avoided colliding with the van by swerving off the road into some shrubs where it became hopelessly stuck. As Paul Sandler looked at the driver, he was surprised to see Roberta Glover, swearing ferociously.

Paul could barely breathe as he considered what he had just done. "Did we rescue a former President of the United States or kidnap Harold Johnson?" he asked Jerome.

"This is the President. I could never forget those eyes," said Jerome. "We're headed to the airport. After I got into the van and briefed the team, I called on the cellular phone to make sure our plane will be ready to take off by the time we arrive. The pilot had already filed a flight plan for Cleveland."

Paul nodded and thought—*I'm glad Jerome knows what to do—they didn't teach this in advanced auditing.*

"By the way, I believe we just alienated *The Washington Globe*. That was Roberta Glover driving, unhurt, but spitting mad," said Sandler.

Jerome laughed, "It's not the first time I've made someone at *The Globe* angry. I'm glad Roberta wasn't hurt. I'm also glad she's stuck in the bushes where she won't get in our way."

Paul's other companions had little idea of what was transpiring, but their orders were to trust Paul's judgment and do whatever he asked, so together, they raced to the airport and the waiting charter plane.

Paul pulled out the cellular phone and called Sidney Harrison.

He explained what he had done and why, concluding with, "I think we rescued the former President of the United States. We're headed for Cleveland, and we need a safe place to land. We don't have a step in the audit program for this circumstance, so I called the firm guru." Paul was somewhat short of breath.

Sidney Harrison was aghast. "You did what?"

Paul repeated, "I think we can get airborne, but I don't know where it's safe to land."

"I'll call back."

At the airport, there were some curious looks at the man in the wheelchair, but Paul and the security team boarded their charter Cessna Citation without incident. Once the plane was aloft, Paul received the call he was waiting for from Sidney Harrison over the secure phone. "I called Governor Jones. He has arranged for you to land at Rickenbacker AFB south of Columbus. He will meet the plane and will have a lot of help with him. By the way, the Governor is trying to arrange an escort, so don't be alarmed if you get some company up there."

"Thanks, Sidney. I have another favor to ask."

"Paul, we are in so deep and I have already pulled so many strings... What do you need?"

"Call John Barlow, the newspaper editor, and ask him to meet us when we land. One of his staff died working on this, and he helped us out. His paper deserves to be there."

"OK. I'll call him. Good luck."

Soon afterward, the pilot opened the sliding door that separates the cockpit from the main cabin and pointed to the right window. Next to their plane was an F-4 Phantom with the words Kansas Air National Guard on the side. The F-4 pilot gave them a thumbs up. The rest of the flight was uneventful, except that the escorts changed each time their plane crossed a state line. *Nice touch, Governor*, thought Paul.

* * * * * *

In the White House, Marian Rose picked up the phone, "Yes, Frank." She listened. "Isn't there anything we can do to stop that plane? I mean anything." After listening again for a long while, she replied in a cold, embittered voice, "I see. Start going through the paper and computer files. Shred or delete everything they can use against us." She then went to a window, sat down in a chair, and stared out onto the White House lawn.

* * * * * *

Upon entering Ohio airspace, their distinguished passenger seemed to become somewhat more alert as the medication began to wear off, though he was still silent.

Jerome looked into the eyes of Alexander Rose and said, "Mr. President. You've been rescued. You're safe now."

The old man stared at Jerome Branson and then began to cry.

Rickenbacker AFB hadn't had a plane land with this much ceremony in some time. The Governor was there with state police, county Sheriff's deputies and City of Columbus policemen. The base commander, the Governor's son-in-law, had Rickenbacker AFB on high alert. That didn't stop John Barlow from managing to get in. He had leased a Lear Jet and was there with a photographer to get a complete account of the entire event.

At a press conference later that day, Governor Jones was asked, "Who were these people who risked their lives to rescue President Rose?"

"Just auditors, who became involved in unusual circumstances and rose to the occasion."

Epilogue

The partners had all gathered in the Dodney, Harrison conference room to watch the resignation speech of Jonathan Rose that was being projected onto a large pull-down screen that hung from the ceiling. Former President Huggard, Marian Rose, and Frank Norman were all under Federal indictment for treason, kidnapping the President of the United States, murder, and plotting to overthrow the government. Former President Alexander Rose was slowly recovering at the Governor's Mansion in Columbus under the care of his old friend, Governor Jones. He could speak haltingly, but would probably never fully recover after such an extended period of sedation.

"I still can't believe that Marian Rose faked the President's death just to stay in power. She must have had lots of help to continue this cover-up for nearly 20 years. More heads are going to roll," Paul ventured.

"No doubt. We are all very proud of what you accomplished, Paul," said Tom Spivey. "I'm glad that the people responsible for Stefie's death are in jail and that you and your family are OK."

"I still don't like governmental audits," John Ryan began lecturing. "In addition to the personal danger, we lost our shirts on this job, what with chartered planes, bodyguards, and time budget overruns. Governmental audits are not profitable. And they're a heck of a lot of trouble."

"Hold on, John," interrupted Sidney Harrison. "I have some news on that score. This afternoon the new administration agreed to reimburse all of our overruns and out-of-pocket expenses, including the airplane and bodyguards. I convinced them that rescuing a former President of the United States is a valid expenditure of the General Fund. But Paul is a true hero regardless of whether or not we get paid. And besides," he added with a smile, "the publicity isn't hurting our firm either."

"Hear, hear," shouted Tom and the partners let out a cheer.

Amid the noise, Tom whispered, "Paul, I've just taken a long-term lease on some office space in Washington. How would you feel about heading up our office there?"

Before a bewildered Paul Sandler could respond, his

friend said, “That’s a joke, Paul. Just a joke.”

About the Authors

Dr. Richard E. Brown and Beverly A. Brown.

Richard Brown received his doctorate at Harvard University's John F. Kennedy School of Government. He has fashioned a career blending both the university and practice worlds. Currently a professor of accounting at Kent State University, he has also taught as a visiting professor at a number of universities, including The College of William and Mary, the State University of New York at Albany, and the University of Kansas. He was also Director of Operational Auditing for Price Waterhouse's Office of Government Services, and before that, appointed Legislative State Auditor of Kansas. Beverly Brown holds degrees in both education and accounting. She has served in teaching and accounting positions for educational, retail, and industrial organizations.